"Should we stop by your home so you can get your swimsuit?"

Olive swung around to face Blake, her face heating. "No, I don't wear anything like that. I mean, Amish don't ever wear them—ever."

"What do you swim in?"

She looked down at her clothes. "Just our clothes."

"Seems as though that would be dreadfully uncomfortable."

Olive shrugged and put the cup under the outlet of the built-in coffee machine. "We don't notice." She turned back toward him once the coffee cup was filled to the brim. "It's not considered modest to show too much skin."

A handsome, wealthy, successful man like Blake would not consider her as a suitable match even if she were *Englisch*.

Men like him weren't likely to be attracted to a nanny, much less an Amish nanny who swam in clothing and closed her eyes to thank *Gott* before every meal.

She wondered what the two of them would have in common or talk about if a marriage between them was ever allowed.

And the more Olive thought about Blake, the faster her heart beat...

Samantha Price wrote stories from a young age, but it wasn't until later in life that she took up writing full-time. Formerly an artist, she exchanged her paintbrush for the computer and, many bestselling book series later, has never looked back. Samantha is happiest lost in the world of her characters. To learn more about Samantha and her books, visit samanthapriceauthor.com.

HIS AMISH NANNY

Samantha Price

ISBN-13: 978-1-335-49969-1

His Amish Nanny

First published in 2018 by Samantha Price.
This edition published in 2019.

Recycling programs for this product may not exist in your area.

This edition published by arrangement with Harlequin Books S.A.

For questions and comments about the quality of this book, please contact us at CustomerService@Harlequin.com.

® and TM are trademarks of Harlequin Enterprises Limited or its corporate affiliates. Trademarks indicated with ® are registered in the United States Patent and Trademark Office, the Canadian Intellectual Property Office and in other countries.

Printed in U.S.A.

HIS AMISH NANNY

Chapter One

Olive Hesh slipped her arms through the sleeves of her green dress, pulled it over her head and smoothed it down with her hands. After putting her white over-apron on, she ran a brush through her long, light brown hair. Once her hair was free of knots, she braided it and pinned it up tightly to fit under her prayer *kapp*.

Her sister ran into her room. "You're going some-where."

She spun around to see Naomi's grim face. "I am. Don't tell *Mamm*."

"I won't. Only if you tell me what you're doing."

"Meeting my friends." Olive turned away from her and resumed her task of getting ready.

Naomi's mouth dropped open. "That's unfair. Can I come?"

Lately, Olive's younger sister was always wanting to tag along. Sometimes Olive allowed her but not that often. It wasn't much fun being among her friends with her sister talking down to her the whole time. Naomi was at that age where she thought she knew everything. "*Nee.* I said I'm seeing my friends. Are you my friend? *Nee!*"

Her younger sister scowled. "Unfair."

"Maybe another time."

"Next time?"

Olive wasn't going to commit to that. "Possibly."

Naomi flopped down on her bed. "You're just going to talk about boys anyway. It'll be as boring as watching fields being plowed."

"We talk about boys because that's the one thing we want, love and marriage. You'll be no different when you grow up."

"That's two things," Naomi blurted out, still in her usual contrary mood.

"*Nee.* It's only the one. You fall in love and marry that person. It's the one act. The thing that'll make our lives complete."

Naomi shook her head. "Sounds boring to me."

"You'll change your mind."

"What if you don't find someone? You've never liked anyone *Mamm's* found for you."

"My taste in men is different from hers."

"You don't want a man like *Dat?* Because Phillip Hegerstein seems very much like *Dat.* He even looks like him."

Olive's nose crinkled at the thought of Phillip. "I want someone different, and amazing, and dreamy."

"He doesn't exist."

Olive frowned at her sister. What if Naomi was right? That was the one thing that scared her. She was never going to settle for the Phillips of this world. Sure, he was okay and would make a suitable husband for someone— someone else, just not for her. "Don't you have chores?"

"Don't be mean."

"Well, you were mean just now saying I'll never marry."

"I'm sorry."

Olive sat down on the bed next to Naomi. "It's just that I hope I won't be forced into a marriage to someone I don't like under the pressure from *Mamm, Dat* and the rest of the community."

"How can someone force you to do that?"

"Not forced exactly, but there is a certain expectation that by a certain age you must do certain things—the same as other people in the community. You'll find out when you get older."

Olive was only thankful she wasn't alone; her four closest friends were in exactly the same place as she in their lives. That took a little pressure off her. If one, or even more so, two of them were to marry that would send her mother into a matchmaking frenzy. Her mother was a competitive woman and had even practiced perfecting the art of making pies until she won first place for taste at the pie drive. The Amish weren't a competitive people so prizes and competitions weren't commonplace with the exception of the once-a-year pie drive that coincided with the annual charity auction.

"I really liked Mark Yoder."

Olive giggled. *Mamm* had invited the visiting Mark Yoder for dinner the week before last.

"What's funny?" Naomi asked.

"He's totally unsuitable for me."

"I thought he was good."

"You should marry him, then, Naomi."

"I'm too young, silly. When I'm old enough, he'll be married already."

As soon as a man from another community visited theirs, Naomi and Olive's mother invited him for dinner. So far, they'd all been unsuitable, but not according to their mother. She'd labeled Olive as fussy, and told her she'd never find a man if she expected someone perfect. Olive was sure that wasn't so. She didn't need a man who was perfect, just the perfect man for her.

Naomi pouted. "Where are you meeting your friends?"

"At the Coffee House, same as always." Olive had kept the same friends since the first day that they started *schul* together; their names were Claire Schonberger, Jessie Miller, Lucy Fuller and Amy Yoder.

"You always go there. Why don't you ever go anywhere else?"

"We like it, that's why. Today's special because I've a plan."

"About what?"

Naomi had never been able to keep quiet about anything. Olive shook her head. "Mmm, I'm not ready to say just yet."

"Why not? That's not fair."

Olive winced at the high-pitched whine in her sister's voice. "I just want to tell them first and then I'll tell you later, how's that?"

"You should tell me first because I'm your *schweschder*."

"Later," Olive stated as firmly as she could because she knew Naomi was prone to nagging.

"What about chores?" Naomi smirked. "I've already done a lot."

Naomi folded her arms. "Do you want me to ask *Mamm* if you've done enough?"

Olive sighed, knowing what Naomi was getting at. "Okay, if I tell you why I'm meeting my friends, will you cover for me?"

A grin bloomed on Naomi's face and she shifted her position. "And will you bring me back something sweet like a chocolate cookie?"

"Okay."

"Tell me then and don't leave anything out."

"I've got a plan I'm going to share with them. None of us has a boyfriend, so I'm going to suggest we get jobs."

Naomi scowled. "Doing what?"

"That's not the point. There are many skills between all of us. Don't you think it's a good idea?"

"It's an idea, but not really a good one if you ask me."

"No one's asking you. Anyway, there's more to it, but you'll only mock me like you always do."

"Humph. You won't forget that chocolate cookie, will you? And if they don't have that, just bring me something yummy."

Olive nodded hoping her friends would like her idea. She'd have to make it sound more enticing than she'd done just now. Olive was determined they should not stay at home and wallow in self-pity while waiting to get married as every other young Amish woman did. No, their lives would be good even if they never found men to marry. With their ages varying between nineteen and twenty, it was odd not one of them within their small group was betrothed.

"I'm riding my bike into town. You make sure *Mamm* doesn't see me. If she notices I'm gone, tell her I won't be long and I had an errand to run."

"What errand? I can't lie."

Frowning at Naomi, she said, "Just tell her I'll explain when I get home. It is an errand anyway, so there!" As Olive walked out of the room, Naomi grumbled about Olive getting to do all the fun things. Even though she'd done plenty of chores for the day, Olive slipped away from the house so her mother wouldn't see her. If *Mamm* saw her heading out, she'd find something else that had to be done, and done at once. It was midday when Olive headed to the barn, got on her bike and headed into town.

Olive's household had three buggies and five buggy horses, but with two of her five older brothers still living at home, the buggies were almost always in use. Her bike was something she could use at any time; and, of course, that mode of transport was approved by the community's bishop.

Olive had arranged with her friends to meet at the coffee shop at one in the afternoon. The fact that most Amish girls of their age were already married with *kinner* and in charge of their own homes had spurred Olive to come up with her plan.

The Coffee House was always the same. It was the largest coffee shop in town and had the name for making the best coffee. It was owned by a local *Englisch* couple and was managed by their son, Dan. The girls had gathered there since they were old enough to go out by themselves. Back then, they had ordered hot cocoas instead of the fancy coffees they loved these days. The tables spilled out onto the sidewalk, for those who wanted to sip their coffees alfresco.

Olive took a seat at their usual table overlooking the

sidewalk. The girls all loved to people-watch as they spent time together.

"Waiting for your friends today, Olive?"

Olive looked up to see Dan towering over her. He was tall, with fair short-cropped hair. Technically, he wasn't handsome, but he had a pleasant and relaxed manner about him. Olive was more than sure that Lucy Fuller had a small crush on him, but love with an *Englischer* could never be pursued. "Hi, Dan. Yes, I'm a little early. They'll be here soon."

"Do you want to wait for them before you order?"

"I'll have one now thanks." She giggled. "And I might have another later."

Dan flashed a smile. He was handsome when he smiled like that. The usual way to order was, "order and pay at the counter," but the five girls always received special treatment from Dan, who rushed to take their orders when they arrived.

"Latte with two shots of caramel, as per usual?"

Olive nodded and, from her table, watched Dan put the order through the system. It was Saturday lunch-time, and the coffee shop would soon be full. Olive hoped she wouldn't have to defend herself against people who wanted to take the chairs away from her table. She pushed the chairs in further to deter anyone from asking her if they were in use. She hated it when that happened.

Claire was the first to arrive. Her warm smile reached her chocolate brown eyes as she reached over to give Olive a quick kiss on her cheek. "So, what are we doing here today?" Claire sat down and smoothed down her dress. "You said you had something exciting to say?"

Olive took a deep breath and let it out slowly while she hoped that they would all think her idea was a good one. "Wait until the others get here and I'll tell you."

Claire and Olive chatted while they waited for the other girls.

One by one, the girls arrived. They always acted as though it had been years since they'd seen each other when in reality it was never more than days.

Lucy strode in, arm in arm with Amy. They looked like they had some scheming of their own going on. The last to arrive was Jessie; she was always fond of making an entrance and thrived on being different from everyone else. And different she was with her striking green eyes and unruly, wavy auburn hair, which she battled continually to keep within her prayer *kapp*.

Dan hurried over with Olive's coffee and took the other orders. Olive was sure that she saw Dan pay Lucy slightly more attention than the other girls, but no one else seemed to notice.

Jessie took advantage of the lull in the conversation when Dan had finished taking the orders. "What is it you've got to tell us, Olive? I'm intrigued. Do you want to start a quilting club or something along those lines? I meant to suggest that we do something of the sort to make the days pass quicker."

Three girls spoke at once on their thoughts of starting a quilting club. Olive let them carry on for a bit and listened to their suggestions, amused that it was nothing like what she had in mind.

When the conversation died down, Amy asked, "Well, is that it, Olive?" When Olive shook her head, Amy asked, "Then tell us! We're all excited to know what you're thinking."

"Okay, listen up. We're done with *schul* ages ago and none of us has anything going for us right now. We aren't getting any younger and nothing is getting any cheaper. I thought it was time to take action toward our futures since none of us has a prospect of marriage."

She watched their faces become serious. Their advancing age and the shortage of marriageable men in the community was a common concern between them now. Being as old as they were, they had to support themselves at least a little so they wouldn't burden their families. None of their parents was wealthy, and they each had to pull their own weight.

It was the no-nonsense Jessie Miller who came straight to the point. "Okay, boss lady, what exactly is your plan? You haven't found someone who will hire all of us, have you?"

They all joked about that scenario being the perfect situation. After all, they enjoyed each other's company and they would work well together. They had been inseparable since they were little girls.

"*Nee*, I haven't found someone to do that, but I do have an idea. I mean, it's worth a shot anyway." The plan had sounded brilliant in her mind, but now after Naomi's reaction, she was a little worried how the girls would react. She had to present her plan clearly.

Olive's family were farmers and had been farmers for generations. When she visited the markets days ago, the idea had come out of nowhere. After two days of research and questioning her *mudder*, who had often sold wares at the farmers market stalls, Olive was ready to tell her friends her idea.

The girls waited as Olive was silent for a moment before she spoke. "The farmers market has tons of foot traffic. Not just regular everyday people, but influential folks. I mean everyone from stay-at-home moms to bank managers. Think of the people who would see us." Olive's words flew out of her mouth with enthusiasm, tumbling over one another.

Lucy interrupted her. "You haven't explained what we're supposed to do."

She was right; Olive had forgotten to explain the full plan. She sighed wishing she was better at speaking in front of others. "We rent out a stall at the market for a week. Instead of selling vegetables or crafts, we sell ourselves. I mean think of it, girls—we sell our services! We're all looking for work."

The girls all exchanged nervous looks and then refocused on Olive. She saw the looks they shared and knew that she had to convince them to trust her. Olive continued to explain, "We each need a job, but so far we've had no success. We're all good at different things, but we can all cook and clean. We advertise ourselves to let people know we're available to work." Olive still saw doubt on their faces, so she turned to Jessie. "Jessie, I know you've been looking for housekeeping jobs. Well, this could be your chance to find someone to hire you. You go out there and be seen; we go to them."

Amy nodded in agreement. "That's right. I like the idea."

"And, what have we got to lose?"

"Amy, you love children. You would be a great nanny, but you've got to get out there so people can meet you. This is a way for people to find out about Amy and the same for each of us."

Jessie cut into Olive's sales pitch. "What if the five of us all look for jobs as maids?"

Claire clapped her hands. "I love it!"

Olive was relieved and then looked at each girl's face and she thought they were in agreement. Olive hoped this idea would be good for all of them. Was it crazy to take out a stall at the farmers' markets in the hope for them all to find jobs?

Lucy said, "I could type up resumes for all of us at the library."

"*Jah*, great idea, *denke*, Lucy." Olive smiled, pleased to see they were warming to her ideas.

Lucy pushed out her chair and stood up. "I'll see if I can borrow pen and paper from Dan and I'll make a few notes."

Lucy's smile at having a quiet word with Dan did not escape Olive's notice.

"Wait. How much is this going to cost?" Jessie asked.

"I talked to them and they said we could have a stall for a week, at the back of the markets, for fifty dollars. That's just ten dollars each."

"That's a lot," Olive heard one of them say.

"Worth it, though, if we get jobs," Jessie countered.

When Lucy came back with a notepad and pen, Olive did her best to convince them. "The stall will cost us ten dollars each a week and won't that be worth it?"

"Okay, I'm in," Lucy had a gleam in her eyes, which Olive guessed was thanks to Dan. At this point, she'd most likely agree to anything.

"Me too," Jessie said.

When everyone had voiced her agreement, Lucy jotted down each girl's particulars for their resumes. After that, Amy helped Lucy add flair to each one. They voted Olive to be in charge of arranging the stall and making up the schedule of who was to be at the stall on each of the days.

Olive rode home and for the first time in her life she felt a sense of freedom. This was the first time she'd made a decision regarding her future rather than floating along with the tide of life.

Once Olive had stored her bike back in the barn, she walked through the door to face her mother glaring at her with hands on hips.

She had remembered her sister's cookie and held it behind her back in a white paper bag. "Hello, *Mamm*. Do you want help with the evening meal?"

"Where have you been?" Her mother tapped the toe of her shoe on the floor. That was never a good sign.

"I've been in town with the girls." Her mother's hands went from her hips to folded across her chest. Swallowing hard, Olive continued, "I'm sorry, *Mamm*, but I was halfway to town when I forgot I should've told you I was going out. I was excited to tell them about my idea—you know the one we discussed?"

Her mother shook her head. "But still, you should've asked. I didn't know you'd gone. I had to go into the barn looking for your bike."

"Hey, *Mamm*." Her younger sister tried to get their mother's attention.

Olive's mother shrugged and glared at Naomi. "Not now."

"Is Olive in trouble again?"

Olive's jaw dropped at her sister's words. "Again? I'm hardly ever in trouble."

"Go sit at the kitchen table ready for some chores," her mother hissed at Naomi. Naomi took two steps back without saying a word then turned and hurried to the kitchen. Now with *Mamm's* attention again on Olive, her face softened. "All I want is for you to tell me where you're going. Is that too much to ask?"

"No, *Mamm*."

"Just because you're an adult doesn't mean you can do what you like; not while you're living under this roof."

Olive nodded. "I won't do it again, *Mamm*."

"Good. Wash up and then help me with the vegetables." Olive walked to the bathroom and was headed off by Naomi. "Did you get it?" Naomi asked.

Olive handed over the cookie and Naomi's face lit up. "*Denke*, Olive. You're the best."

"Just eat it quickly."

"I will."

"Naomi!" *Mamm* yelled.

"Gotta go." Naomi hid the cookie under her apron and raced back to the kitchen.

Olive was upset with herself for not telling her mother she was going to town. She wouldn't have stopped her, but she might've found one or two more chores for her before she left. It had been a calculated decision on Olive's part; one she now regretted. It seemed, despite her objection to Naomi, she was always in trouble over something.

After Olive had washed her hands, she sat down with her mother to shell the mountain of peas on the table. "I love fresh peas."

"Well, no eating while shelling because they're for dinner."

"*Jah, Mamm*."

"How did your idea go over with your friends?" Her mother raised an eyebrow.

"They love the idea. One of the girls is doing everyone's resumes on the computer and we're seeing about renting a stall at the farmers market to promote ourselves."

"Good."

Olive smiled at her mother. "*Denke* for helping me come up with the idea."

"It was your idea, Olive. I just listened while you decided on it. You're just like your *vadder* in that regard. You've got a lively and industrious mind."

"Denke, Mamm."

"And you'll get a job that suits you. With actions and prayers, miracles happen. My only hope is one day you'll set your mind on finding a husband with as much gusto."

Olive quickly popped one of the peas into her mouth. "I hope so. Wait." She looked across at her mother. "What?"

Her mother shook her head. "Never mind."

"I told you," Naomi whispered to Olive.

"You told her what?" *Mamm* frowned.

Naomi licked her lips that were dusted with cookie crumbs. "I told Olive you'd find her a good man."

Mamm's frown was replaced with a grin. "If she doesn't find one for herself pretty soon, it'll be up to me."

Chapter Two

When the first day of their week at the farmers market came, the girls were all excited. They had decided beforehand to break up the week into shifts and have two people in the stall at all times. Olive and Lucy were scheduled for the first day. Even though they all wanted jobs as maids, each girl had special skills. Claire was a brilliant cook, Amy was good with children, Olive was a great organizer, Jessie loved to garden, and Claire and Lucy had experience with the sick as they had both taken care of sick, elderly relatives.

Olive had brought along sandwiches and juice to sustain herself and Lucy throughout the day. From the beginning of the day, Olive knew it had been a good idea. Their resume flyers were being scooped up and the first reaction from passersby was positive.

The day had been quite warm and their budget had only permitted an outside stall, and being in the bright sun with no shade made Olive grateful she was only going to be there for two more days.

They had handed out dozens of flyers, but there had been no takers. Olive was starting to lose hope. Two hours before closing, Olive's father stopped by. Olive stepped out to talk to him privately and left Lucy to staff the stall.

"Don't look so down, Olive. It's a good sign no one has offered to employ any of you yet. It only means people are taking you seriously and thinking long and hard about what each of you has to offer. You've put the effort in and no effort goes unrewarded."

Olive smiled and nodded. He was always encouraging to his *kinner*. "*Denke, Dat*, I'm not feeling down, I just hoped that one of us would get a job on the first day. We've got the stall for a week, and there are five of us, so I was hoping that things might have happened quicker."

"Always trying to force things aren't you." He put both hands on Olive's shoulders. "Let things happen in *Gott's* timing."

Olive looked back at her stall. "Do you think that this was a bad idea, *Dat*?"

"*Nee,* I don't think it was a bad idea." He lowered his head leaning toward her. "You don't need to work; we don't need the money. I'd be happy to have you to stay at home until you get married, and have you help your *mudder* until then."

Olive frowned, knowing things weren't as rosy as he said. They did need extra money. "*Dat*, I don't want to move out from home, but I want to pay my way. Who knows what might happen in the future, and what if I never marry? There are too many women in the community and not enough men."

"Have faith, Olive."

His words were full of faith, but his eyes told another story. He knew there were only two men their ages and that was her own brother, Elijah, and Jessie's brother, Mark. Olive's other brother who lived at home was betrothed to a woman from a different community. Olive had no interest in Mark and, for some reason, not one of her friends liked her brother in that way. "Okay, I will. You don't mind me getting a job though?"

He adjusted his straw hat. "*Nee*, if that's what you want to do and if your *mudder* is all right with it."

Olive nodded. "She is."

"Do you want me to wait around for you to finish up?"

"*Nee, denke.* Lucy's going to drive me home." Olive nodded toward Lucy who was now busy speaking to an older couple who'd stopped by the stall.

Olive's father nodded and went about his business picking up a few things from the markets for the family since *Mamm* always said she was too busy to leave the home. Olive's family was nearly self-sufficient, but they still needed some things from the markets.

None of the girls had been successful in getting a job the first day, and now it was Tuesday at two in the afternoon. Olive was growing tired.

Just get to the end of the day.

At least it wasn't as hot as the day before. Her friend Jessie was supposed to have joined her that morning, but she was still nowhere in sight. It wasn't like her to be unreliable and Olive knew something must've happened.

A little while later, a well-dressed lady walked past holding the hand of a toddler. The lady looked at Olive and Olive smiled at her. Then Olive couldn't keep her eyes from the handsome boy with his blonde curls.

Without warning, the boy lunged at the resumes from Olive's stall and threw them to the ground.

"Leo, stop it, at once." The woman made a grab for him, but the boy was too quick.

He jumped on Olive's papers then ran away. Perched on her stiletto heels, the woman made a good effort to catch up to him but failed. Olive covered her mouth in shock. She wasn't used to children who were not well behaved. Amish children were always obedient and polite even at a young age. With their strict discipline, they dared not be anything else. This boy darted the opposite way avoiding the older woman.

Olive stepped in front of the boy who'd spun around and was now heading her way. He stopped in his tracks, and then she crouched down. "Hello, what's your name?"

He promptly poked out his tongue.

Olive ignored his antics and did her best not to laugh. "I think I can pick up these papers faster than you." Olive reached out her hand to pick up the papers.

"No, me." The boy grabbed them before she got them. "I do it," the toddler mumbled.

"No. I'll do it," Olive said.

"No, me." The little boy proceeded to gather all the papers he had thrown. Once he'd picked up all the papers, he handed them to Olive.

"Why thank you; that's very nice of you. Did you say your name was Michael?"

The little boy giggled and shook his head. "What about David, is that your name?"

The little boy giggled again, and said, "I'm Leo."

"Oh, Leo. Well, it's nice to meet you. I'm Olive."

While Olive was still crouched on the ground, he

flung his arms around her neck and nearly knocked her over, and would have if she hadn't managed to grab onto the table.

The older woman seized the opportunity to take hold of the boy's arm. "Thank you. I'm terribly sorry for what my grandson has done. I don't know what gets into him sometimes." He struggled to get out of her grasp, but the woman kept a firm hold.

"Full of beans they are at that age." Olive stood up. Leo managed to squirm away from his grandmother and grabbed Olive's hand. Olive giggled. "Seems I've made a friend."

"It appears you have." The older lady stepped to one side, picked up one of the flyers and read it. "Are you looking for a job?"

"Yes, I'm looking for a job as a maid. My four friends are as well. We each have a different specialty." The woman looked wealthy, judging from her clothing, and with her brightly painted long nails she didn't look like she did her own cleaning. "Are you looking for a house-keeper?"

"Well, my son, Leo's father, needs a nanny. I've told him I can't keep looking after the boy. You've seen how he is and I'm too worn out for all that now at my age. I've been there and done that and I'm not enjoying being forced to do it all over again."

"My good friend, Amy Yoder, is good with children." With Leo still having a firm grip on Olive's hand, she used her free hand to sort through the papers to find Amy's resume.

The woman didn't even look at the resume once Olive found it and held it out to her. "What about you?"

"I can clean. I'm looking for a job as a maid."

"What about looking after children?"

"I could do that, but Amy's so much better at it than I am." She stared into Olive's eyes for a moment and then shook her head. "No, I want you for the job. You'd be perfect and in between times, you could do a little tidying up for my son."

Olive stood tall. "I have had some experience, but what I've had is with my younger sister, and nieces and nephews."

"See? That's all the experience you need. Sounds like you're a natural."

Olive wondered if this whole thing of renting the stall at the farmers market was a good idea after all. Was she getting in way over her head? "I do have a first-aid certificate," Olive said, mostly to make herself feel more qualified. "Um, because I was helping out at the volunteer firefighters and I thought why not find out—"

"Splendid. The job pays well and I'll make sure you're paid a week in advance. All you have to do is keep Leo occupied. You don't have to shop or clean. Blake has someone clean the house once a week and the food is delivered weekly as well."

This is all happening fast. Was she getting a real job? Could it all be this easy or would Leo's father see she was a fraud?

"I'll write down his address. Is seven o'clock in the morning too early for you? I know he leaves for work around eight and he'll probably want to run through a few things with you." The older lady rattled around in her bag until she found a pen. She wrote down a name, address and phone number. "My name is Sonia Worthington and my son is Blake. I can't wait to tell Blake about you; he'll be so pleased I found a nanny, finally."

"I'm not a real nanny, though. I've got no real experience; I just wanted a job as a maid."

"Do you want a full-time job?"

Olive quickly thought what she could do with the money from full-time employment. She could save it for her future as well as contribute to the household budget. If she never married, she wanted to have her own home rather than have to live with one of her siblings as a sad old maid. "Full-time would be good. You want me to start tomorrow?"

"You can, can't you? I've got a bridge game tomorrow. If I have to look after Leo again, I'll have to cancel. Then after that, I've got my hair appointment with Maxwell Leon. I've had that appointment booked for four weeks; he's so hard to get into. He's an excellent colorist. A friend recommended him and I was lucky he accepted me." Sonia looked at Olive's prayer *kapp*. "I guess you've no need for a hair care specialist?"

Olive touched her fingertips to her prayer *kapp* and looked at the blonde hair piled high on Sonia's head. "No, I don't. Not really. Yes, tomorrow is fine." Olive took the information from Sonia, recognized the street name and was pleased that it wasn't too far from town. It was close enough that she could ride her bike. "Nice and close." Olive smiled. "Are you sure this will be okay with your son? I mean, he's never met me."

"It'll be okay. I make most of the decisions for him; he's so busy. He works far too much."

Leo squealed about something, let go of Olive's hand and his little chubby legs ran. Sonia dashed to grab his arm and this time she was successful. She turned back to Olive. "Thank you, Olive. I'll see you again."

"Yes. And I'll be there tomorrow. Thank you very much, Sonia."

Olive's eyes fixed upon Sonia and Leo as they disappeared down one of the lanes. Leo needed discipline; he wasn't a bad child. Olive knew that every child needed structure and discipline and it seemed to Olive that Leo lacked both of those. She wondered why Leo's mother wasn't mentioned. Were Leo's parents divorced?

An hour before the farmers markets closed for the day, Jessie rushed toward the stall. "I'm so sorry, Olive. There was an accident, and my *bruder* broke his leg. He was fixing something on the roof, and he slipped off. He's still in the hospital."

"That's awful, Jessie! He'll be alright, won't he?"

"It was a bad break, but I guess he's lucky he didn't do any more damage. A tree broke his fall."

Jessie's parents' *haus* was two full stories, so her *bruder* would have fallen from quite a height. "You need not have come in at all, Jessie."

"I said I'd be here. I always do what I say. Even though I'm a bit late I made it." Jessie gave a sharp nod of her head to emphasize her point.

Olive touched Jessie lightly on her arm. "Do you want me to get you a cup of tea or something?"

Jessie shook her head. "I'm okay. I had too many *kaffes* in the hospital while we were waiting for the X-rays and when we were waiting for the cast. He'll be back home tonight, they said."

"Sit down while I give you some good news." Olive pulled a small chair out from under the table and when Jessie sat down, she told her the news of her new job.

Jessie clapped her hands. "You were right to do this. We'll all have jobs soon. I'm so pleased for you, Olive."

"*Denke.* Well, we'll have to re-arrange the schedule since it looks like I won't be here for the rest of the week. I was going to help out on Thursday, but now I won't be able to."

"I'll arrange it with the others; you just concentrate on your new job. I didn't know you wanted to work with children; I thought that's what Amy wanted to do."

"I tried to tell the lady about Amy, but she said the little boy got on well with me, so she wanted me." Olive breathed out heavily.

"What's the matter? You look upset now."

"The *grossmammi* hired me, but the catch is that the boy's father knows nothing of me. How do I know I'm not going to show up at the house for nothing? I might be back here after all. It's not as though one of the boy's parents hired me."

Jessie drew her chin in toward her chest. "*Nee*, surely not. She would have had the 'say so' otherwise she would not have given you the job."

"*Jah*, you're right. I'm probably worrying about nothing. I hope Amy's not mad with me. Anyway, it's not my turn on the stall tomorrow. If I go there and have to leave right away, it doesn't matter. In a way, I've got nothing to lose." Olive noticed Jessie's face was pale and more hair than usual was poking out from underneath her *kapp*. She looked a bit of a mess. "You go home, Jessie. I'll be finished up soon; there probably won't be many people interested in hiring a maid or a nanny this late in the day."

"I feel terrible for letting you down today, Olive."

"Nonsense. Family comes first. Go and look after that *bruder* of yours and make sure he stays on the ground."

Chapter Three

"We're home!" Sonia called out in a singsong voice as she made her way into the house. "And someone better be home because someone forgot to lock the door again."

Sonia held the door for Leo as he toddled into the house with an oversized brown bag balanced in his arms. "Well, thank you kindly, good sir! You are such a big help bringing in those vegetables for me."

Leo's face beamed in response as he looked up at her from under his blonde curls. Sonia noted it was near time for him to get another haircut. She would have to remind Blake to do that; she had done her duty long enough, looking after Leo every day for the past months.

Leo pulled out an ear of corn from the bag he dropped on the kitchen floor. "Can I eat it?"

"Maybe for dinner," Sonia said. "I would love some good fresh corn too. We have to cook it first though."

"Hey there!" A deep voice greeted them.

Sonia looked up to see her son striding down the hall. "I thought I heard voices out here," Blake said.

"Only a couple vandals out to rob you while you're busy in your den with the front door unlocked," Sonia chided Blake lightly, as she gave him a peck on the cheek in greeting. "You need another pair of hands around here, honey. You're starting to get absent-minded."

"Working on that, Mom, but I'm home so that's why I didn't lock the door." Blake took another bag of groceries from his mother. Then he leaned over to take the bag his son had dumped on the floor. "How'd you do today, champ? Want me to take that?"

"No! I want it!" Leo hugged the ear of corn and shuffled his way out of the kitchen.

Blake watched him leave. "He looks tired. What did you two get up to today?"

"Leo made a friend at the farmers market." Sonia chuckled at Blake's perplexed expression. "He got a few good words of wisdom from a very nice lady. She was a young lady, and pretty too. I think it was good fortune for both of us that we went there today."

"Sorry to have Leo joining you on errands, Mom. I'm working to find him a good nanny as soon as possible. Now, I know that you said you'd look after him, but I also know it hasn't been easy. I can see the tension on your face."

"Do I have wrinkles? Can you see any?" She pulled a mirrored compact from her bag. This was the worst news ever. In the afternoon daylight, she saw those pesky crows' feet. Even the Botox hadn't been able to eliminate them completely. When she had asked for more Botox on the crows' feet, she'd found that the skin underneath her eyes had become wrinklier. All she could do was not think about them. Perhaps the answer was a full facelift. She swung around to look at her only son.

"Mom, I will find someone. I'm sorry I've left you for so long with him."

"Oh, don't worry about that. You've got enough to think about. I've loved having him with me."

"Loved?" Blake drew his dark brows together. "I'll get a nanny soon, okay?"

Sonia waved his question away with a swipe of her hand then decided it was time to tell him what she had planned. He'd find out soon enough and this time she wouldn't let him boss her about like he did his employees. She'd been reluctant to tell him because he had a history of flying into a temper when things went the wrong way. "Since you've just brought up the subject of a nanny, I've got some great news for you."

He folded his arms across his broad chest. "News?" He chuckled. "The markets had a good special today? I know how you love bargains. Did you buy another handbag?"

"You can't get the handbags I like at the markets, dear. I shop in New York City." She rolled her eyes. If he paid more attention to her, he'd know where she bought accessories.

"What's the news then?" Blake asked, now appearing to be half listening to his mother as he went in search of where Leo had run off to with the corn.

"Oliff!" Leo crowed triumphantly as he ran out from his downstairs bedroom toward his father.

"Oliff? What's he trying to say, Mom? He's been speaking so clearly lately—now he's back to the baby-talk." Blake's eyes widened slightly and he caught himself with a relieved smile. "Oh, you bought olives at the food markets. I love olives."

"No!" Leo said, looking at his dad with a very familiar impatient expression. "Oliff is a lady."

"Yes. We found a lady called Olive at the markets didn't we, Leo?" Sonia beamed as she took off her soft, pink leather jacket. "Now, I think it's time for the cartoons, isn't it, Leo?"

"Mom, you know I don't like him sitting in front of the television all day."

The diamonds on her fingers flashed as Sonia once again waved a manicured hand in the air. "Relax! It won't hurt for a little bit. I've got something to tell you and I can't tell you while Leo's screaming the house down." Sonia turned to her grandson. "Cartoons, Leo?" Leo made a dash for the living room.

"Oh, no." Blake managed to beat Leo to the remote for the flat screen, saving it from smudges of sticky fingers.

Once the television was set up with cartoons and Leo sat transfixed by the colorful characters, Blake walked toward his mother. Sonia busied herself putting away the vegetables hoping he was going to accept Olive as a nanny. It was her only way to escape the boredom of looking after a child all day. Her friends only saw their grandchildren once or twice a month and that was what Sonia wanted. She smiled when she looked up to see Blake's worried face.

"What do you have to tell me, Mother?"

"Before you get angry just hear me out. I hired a nanny and she starts tomorrow."

"What? You what?" Blake collapsed heavily onto one of the stools pushed up against the granite kitchen island. "Why so suddenly; couldn't we have talked about this first?"

Sonia turned, shut the refrigerator door and put one hand on her hip. "Do try to be more open-minded, darling. You've had those names from the employment agencies for months and you've done nothing about them."

Blake narrowed his eyes at her. "Please tell me you're joking."

"You look just like your father when you stare at me like that."

"What's wrong with my father?"

Sonia rolled her eyes. "Don't get me started on that one. Anyway, you should have seen Olive with Leo. He was throwing things, jumping on things and running away and with a few quiet words from her, he turned into an angel. Did I mention she's attractive?" She thought that might change his stubborn opinion. "When I found out she was looking for a job, it was obvious what the next step had to be."

"Was it?" Now his teeth were gritted.

"Of course, darling. It simply made sense that she was the perfect person to look after him. Someone has to manage him." Blake's wife had been an artist and a hippie and her ideas had rubbed off on Blake. "I know you believe in him being a free spirit and all that and having that artistic flair, but he needs a firm hand and I can't be that to him. I just want to be his loving grandmother, not his sitter."

"I know he needs firmness. When I said I wanted him to be able to think for himself, I meant when he was older. I don't know where you get the 'free spirit' nonsense from. I never said that, not once."

"He takes after you. You were a handful too when you were his age. I thought I could manage him every day and I want to, but I can't. I've things to do, putting it simply, and looking after a grandson every single day of the week does not fit in with my lifestyle." She watched Blake's hurt expression. "At this stage of my life, I'm entitled to some *me* time. I've raised a child; I've been there, done that. I have no wish to do it all over again. I don't know how many lunches and functions I've had to turn down."

Blake leaned on the kitchen island and rubbed his forehead. "I knew it would be too much for you. Thank you for trying. It means a great deal. But, you could have let me find a nanny."

"Do you have coffee made?"

"No. Who is this person you hired?" Blake asked. "You always do this, Mother. You always decide what's best for me without even asking me. Why couldn't you have waited and asked me about it first?"

"You would have said no." Sonia tried to sound firm despite her son's glowering expression. "Your new nanny is a lovely young lady. Olive Hesh is her name."

Blake sighed in exasperation. "The agency sent me loads of resumes, over a month ago. I could've chosen one of them."

"My point exactly. You don't want a nanny, or you would've chosen one. You must be practical. Leo needs consistency in his life. Leo and I hired one for you. Problem solved!" Sonia smiled as she checked the coffee pot. "I know you were set on finding a perfect nanny, but as it turns out, she found us. It really couldn't have worked out more perfectly."

"Mom, I just wish you would have checked with me

first. I can't have someone I've never met look after Leo.
I haven't even had time to arrange the internal security
cameras. I'll have to call this nanny you found for me
and cancel her employment."

"No, you will not!" He was pushing her about just as
his father used to and she would not have it. He didn't
need to spy on Olive. Sonia knew that in her heart.

He stared at his mother in disbelief. "Okay, to be fair,
I'll have her come for an interview first."

"Yes, yes, but then you'll put the whole thing off. It
would have taken over a year with you being the per-
fectionist you are." Sonia poured two cups, waving him
off as he tried to take over. "I've got this, sit back down.
Come on now, just relax. She's perfect for the job. You'll
love her. I personally guarantee it."

Blake took a slow breath while his mother poured
his coffee. There were moments when his mother went
too far with her controlling—even if well intended—
ways. "Would you please start at the beginning? Where
did you meet this woman? What are her qualifications?
For whom has she worked previously? Has she worked
for any of your friends?" His mother took a sip of coffee. "Leo and I were at the markets as I said. And he
started into a fit about something or other. He was trying to drag me off to see something he'd spotted. I
thought we would have to leave he was making such
a scene. People were staring." Sonia raised a finger to
stop Blake as he opened his mouth. "Don't start on his
behavior; we're talking about something more important at the moment."

Blake nodded and kept quiet.

"Anyway, this darling young lady came over and

started talking to Leo. She crouched down and chattered with him about how boring shopping can be and asked him what his name was. I couldn't really hear too much of what they were talking about, but he took to her instantly. He was an angel the rest of our trip."

"She works there? So, she runs a fruit stall or some such, and you think she's capable of looking after Leo?"

"Now don't huff and puff so. She explained she and a couple of friends are out of work and they set up a stall to advertise themselves in the hope of finding jobs."

"How industrious of them."

"Exactly what I thought. It shows that they're hard working and you have to admire their resourcefulness."

"I don't need a woman with entrepreneurial skills, I just need a nanny. Please tell me she has some experience at least. Does she have a degree in child psychology at least?"

"She's a nanny not an academic. You've got to be realistic. She was looking for a job as a housekeeper."

Blake pressed his lips together. He didn't want to get too angry with his mother; she was genuinely trying to help. She truly believed that the girl would do a good job.

"Leo doesn't usually take to people so quickly. So, I asked if he wanted her to look after him and he said yes. I did ask him after I asked her, of course."

Blake gasped and sputtered, ignoring the coffee that was growing cold in front of him. "Mother, I'm trying very hard not to get angry. I can't get my head around the idea that you hired a strange woman that neither of us knows just because she spoke nicely to Leo. Even though he's so advanced in many ways, he's only just turned two and he wouldn't know what's good for him or who's best to look after him."

"Oh, it was much more than that. I have a good feeling about this one. She will be an absolute dream. Don't worry about the salary. I'll pay her wages, so don't fret about the money."

"No, Mother. I can afford to hire a nanny for my own son."

"And fire her?" Sonia asked with a knowing smile. "Relax, darling. You can take over her salary after she's been here a while if you like. I know you well enough not to leave her in your hands with your fifty excuses not to even try."

"I'll need my police friend, Doug Briggs, to run a background check on her. What's her name again?"

"Blake James William Worthington, you'll do no such thing. You can't do something like that without asking a person. Anyway, she told me she has many brothers and sisters who she looked after. I think it was six she said she had. Maybe four, or it could've been six younger brothers and sisters. You can't get better on the job training than that. Those nannies you're considering might never have changed a diaper in their lives. You can't learn about kids from a classroom and an exam. Papers don't give you a personality either."

"Mother, this is insane. I will not choose a nanny on someone's personality. I hope you didn't either."

"It's what people have done for hundreds of years. Find a nice woman who knows kids and hire them. It's not that difficult, dear. Millions of children have survived the process." She smiled in that calm, stubborn way that told Blake that no matter what he said or did, the matter was settled. Nothing would change her mind or stop Sonia from having her way on this one.

"Trust me, dear. I have a great feeling about this one. Mother knows best."

"Right," Blake grumbled. He took a sip of his coffee, which had grown cold. He hoped this new excuse for a nanny would not prop his son in front of the television all day. His mother meant well, but how would he go to work tomorrow knowing that a stranger with minimal experience would be in charge of the most precious person in his life? It was absurd. "How about this? I'll try her out for a day, but you must be here in the house the whole time and never leave her unattended with Leo. There's no way I'm leaving a complete stranger with him."

"Okay."

"Good." That would give him time to get his security team to hook up nanny cams throughout the house. He'd make a call and have them installed tomorrow evening when he was there to supervise the installation.

"We have a deal then?" His mother stuck out her hand.

He looked down at her hand and then up into her face. "Just for one day with you here and you'll never take your eyes off Leo?"

His mother nodded. "Absolutely, agreed."

"Deal." He took her hand and shook it.

Chapter Four

Olive sat up in bed, stretched her hands over her head and yawned. She'd had a good sleep and was excited to start her new day, which would be her first day of work as a nanny. If Leo's father was as nice as Leo's grandmother, working for that family would be wonderful. The accidental meeting with Leo's grandmother had to have been arranged by God, she reasoned.

She exchanged her nightdress for one of her old dresses, a dark green one. She knew that playing with children could get messy and Sonia had mentioned she might have to do a little tidying and she wouldn't want to do that in her Sunday best. She brushed out her long hair, divided it into two sections and plaited them. Then she pinned the braids against her head and put on her prayer *kapp*. Normally, she let the strings hang, but since she was going on the bicycle today, she tied the strings under her chin. When she had pulled on her stockings and her shoes, she headed downstairs to do her chores before she set out.

Naomi had the chores of collecting eggs and feeding the chickens, while she had the jobs of making a cooked breakfast for the family and doing whatever else *Mamm* told her.

When she got to the kitchen, her father and two of her brothers, Elijah and Thomas, were back from the morning milking, sitting at the breakfast table waiting.

Elijah sat with his hands around a mug of coffee. "Take extra time to get ready this morning, did you?"

"Oh, I didn't realize I was late. Where's *Mamm*?"

"Should be down in a minute," her father said.

Olive wasted no time putting on the breakfast for the hungry workers who had already put in hours of work doing the morning milking.

"*Mamm* tells me you're starting work today, Olive," Thomas said.

"*Jah*, that's right."

Dat frowned. "You didn't mention that over dinner last night."

"Oh, it's not a secret. *Mamm* knew. I don't know why she didn't say anything about it."

"Nervous, are you?" Elijah asked.

"Um, maybe a little bit. I think I'm more excited. I'm nanny for a lovely little boy. He's very lively and his grandmother had a bit of trouble controlling him."

Dat chuckled. "Sounds like you might have a bit of a challenge there."

"I don't know. We'll see."

"How are you getting there?" Elijah asked. "I hope you don't want me to take you there because you should've asked me yesterday."

Thomas said, "And I can't because I'm meeting Mandy at her place to go over wedding plans."

"It's close enough for me to ride my bike," Olive said.

Her father leaned toward her. "Make sure you write

the address down for us before you leave. We need to know where you are."

"Of course. I can do that." She placed bacon strips in the sizzling-hot frying pan. The usual breakfast was bacon and eggs with hash browns. She didn't know how the men could eat so much, but she knew it was tiring milking the cows twice a day, and she was sure the three of them did the work of four men. Somehow, they managed.

Even though she had a full day's work ahead of her, Olive had done her fair share of chores before she left the house. She rode her bike directly to the address she'd been given by Sonia, and when she arrived, she looked up at the house and double-checked the address. She had the right place, but she hadn't expected the house to be so grand. It looked a little out of place for the general locality. She climbed off her bike and opened the large gates, wheeled her bike through and automatically went back to close the gates. Olive had been trained to always close gates on the farm. Then she walked her bike to the side of the house and leaned it against the wall.

It all made sense; Sonia's son was just as wealthy as his mother. Even at the farmers market, Mrs. Worthington had been covered in diamonds, and no doubt, designer clothes. They had to be wealthy for Sonia to offer the kind of money she'd mentioned.

The yard was beautifully landscaped and looked as if it was a park rather than a private yard. Olive wondered if Sonia's son took care of it himself or whether he had a gardener. No, Sonia mentioned that her son worked all the time, so he most likely employed a gardener. It had to take a considerable amount of time to keep the flowerbeds and hedges in such exact and pristine shape.

Sonia had made no mention of Leo's mother, so Olive figured that her son was most likely divorced, or maybe a widower. The reality of her new job caused Olive's heart to pound in her ears as she hesitated at the back door. *Keep it together, Olive.* Steadying herself with a deep breath, she pressed the doorbell.

It seemed that this man, Blake, wanted his mother to look after his young boy, but Sonia had other priorities. Olive giggled to herself about Leo's behavior the day before; she was used to young children and knew how to distract them. She had a theory that children generally misbehaved to gain attention.

After a reasonable amount of time had ticked by, she pressed the doorbell again. When there was still no response, she called out, "Hello?"

"Come in," she heard a male voice say from somewhere within the house.

She opened the door, walked in and looked around and saw no one. She walked further inside, and her breath caught in her throat when she saw the kitchen. It was straight out of one of the designer magazines she often flipped through at the coffee shop. It was all dark wood and glossy, with white stone countertops and gleaming stainless-steel appliances.

She secretly couldn't wait until she could cook something in there. Olive snapped out of it and wondered where Leo and his father were. She moved silently through the house toward Leo's squeals until she could tell that they were coming from the next level. She stopped at the bottom of the wide staircase when she heard Leo's feet come padding down.

"Leo, Leo, stop running!" Blake yelled from behind his son.

Olive moved quickly to intercept the little boy when he reached the bottom of the staircase. She held her arms out wide and scooped him up. Leo squealed louder as she swung his little body around in a circle. She was so distracted by his happy smiling face that she momentarily forgot about the boy's father.

Blake stood at the bottom of the stairs and looked her up and down. "I'm sorry; I thought you were someone else. I'm not interested in any religious chatter, and I'm getting ready for work. And, yes, I'm saved." Blake motioned toward the door. "I'll walk you out."

Standing still, Olive opened her mouth in shock. "Didn't your mother mention me?"

He raised his dark eyebrows. "You…no…you're the nanny?"

"Yes." Olive relaxed the tension that had suddenly built up in her shoulders and set Leo back on his feet. Sonia had told him she was coming.

"You're Amish," he said in an accusatory tone.

Olive smiled at him. "Yes, I am."

"And you're my mother's idea of the perfect nanny?"

"She said that?" Olive tried to pay attention even though Leo was tugging at the bottom of her dress.

Blake crossed his arms and studied her through narrowed eyes.

"Oliff, Daddy." Leo was ignored by his father.

The man couldn't have made it more obvious she wasn't welcome.

She ignored his wariness and put out her hand. "Hello, I'm Olive Hesh."

His handshake was firm and his skin was velvet soft,

not like the harsh callused hands she knew most of the Amish farm boys would have.

"Blake Worthington, and I understand you're already acquainted with my son." He glanced down at Leo.

"I do hope it's all right me being here. Sonia seemed pleased to have me watch Leo." She felt a clench of anxiety at his doubtful expression. It was clear he did not share his mother's enthusiasm, which caused Olive's smile to falter.

"You're early. Sorry about before, but I've never had much to do with the Amish. When I saw you just inside the door, I thought you'd come to save me from—well, save me from myself."

Olive felt heat rise in her cheeks. "We don't push our beliefs onto others. And I'm sorry if I caught you at a bad time. I always try to be a little early. It's a habit that I got from my parents; they always have to be ten or fifteen minutes early wherever they go."

"No," he said, "that's fine. I like people to be on time. People don't value time nowadays. I subscribe to the notion that time is money."

"I know what you mean." Olive relaxed enough to notice that he was a handsome man and so tall that he towered above her.

Sonia hadn't said what her son did for a living, but he did not have the build of an office worker. His hard body resembled someone who worked hard for a living, such as a farmer or a construction worker. However, he wore a white business shirt and dark gray suit pants, so it seemed his job was an office job of sorts. It was not the time to ask him what kept him away from his son every day.

"Olive, I need to talk to you about this arrangement."

"Ollie, Oliff!" Leo cheered as he wrapped himself around her legs in an excited hug before grabbing her hand to drag her further into the house. "Play, Oliff! Come to my room!"

"I'd love to!" Olive knelt down, so she was eye to eye with the boy. "But first, I need to talk to your daddy for a moment. Would you be a dear and set up the first game you want to play while he and I talk?"

"I wanna play now!" Leo's voice began lilting upward into a whine.

Blake frowned and gently laid a hand on his son's shoulder and opened his mouth to speak, but Olive was quick to say, "Grown-ups talk first and then we'll play. Now, you wait for me in your room." Olive's tone was firm but nice.

Leo turned and toddled slowly to his room.

Blake watched his son walk away, and said with pride, "He's just turned two. He talks so well for his age."

Olive said, "Yes. Some children aren't even talking at that age."

"If I'd said that he wouldn't have listened. I see he listens to you." He stared at Olive.

"He does. You wanted to speak to me?"

"Yes, come and sit in the kitchen please, if you don't mind."

While they sat, Olive studied his face. His jawline was strong, his nose was nicely shaped and not too big and his lips were full but masculine. His eyes were as dark as his hair and his face was clean-shaven. After Blake still hadn't said anything, Olive asked, "What was it you wanted to speak to me about?"

"Oh, yes." He coughed and glanced at his wristwatch. "I want to make it clear this arrangement is temporary. A trial run, if you will. You'll be paid of course."

She nodded. "Yes, Sonia, um, your mother, made it clear yesterday."

"She said nothing of a trial period."

Olive did not want to get his mother into trouble and by the frown on Blake's brow, it looked as though that was in danger of happening. "I was a little distracted by your beautiful son and his fair hair. I don't fully remember the exact conversation."

Blake's face softened, and he gave a low chuckle. "His hair used to be long and curly, but we had to have it cut because everyone thought he was a girl. He can be distracting. Everyone makes such a fuss of his looks that I think Leo is certain he can get away with anything."

"I assure you I won't let him misbehave. My parents were strict and firm, but also kind and fair." Olive gave a quick nod of her head.

Blake's lips turned upward at the corners. "And how old are you? Normally, I wouldn't ask a lady her age, but I guess I'm entitled to know in circumstances such as these."

Olive tilted her chin upward. "I'll be twenty soon, Mr. Worthington."

He visibly winced and shook his head. "Blake, just Blake, please. I always think people are referring to my late father when they call me Mr. Worthington."

"Sorry." She gave him a smile. "I can't promise I'll always catch myself though. It tends to be a habit. My family is old fashioned when it comes to respecting elders."

"Heavens, I'm not that old."

"Sorry." She lowered her head hoping that she

would not have to watch what she said every single day. "Maybe I should have said, 'employers' instead."

"Nothing wrong with respect," he affirmed as he checked his watch once more. "I'm trying to get Leo on a schedule, but Mom's let that slip by the wayside. He needs a timetable, a regular schedule. The emergency contact numbers are on the fridge." He stood up. "I'll show you where Leo's room is before I go to work, and my mother will be here with you for your first day—your trial day. She's due any minute."

"Yes, Mr. Worthington, I mean, Blake," she corrected herself in a quick breath. He stared at her as she gave him a light apologetic look. "I did say it was a habit!"

"I'm sorry if I appeared to be a little short with you earlier. I was shocked my mother employed a nanny on my behalf without prior discussion. I can't make any promises to keep you on, but since you're already here, it'll be a trial for today."

Olive was confused; didn't he just say he'd give her a short trial period, now it was just for today? It seemed he'd made up his mind about her already, and not in a good way. "Sonia assured me this would be a full-time position. I can understand that you might want to give me a trial period of say, two weeks?"

Blake breathed out heavily and put his fingertips to his forehead, covering his eyes as if he had a headache coming on. "Very well, very well. But it'll be *one* week and I'll see how we all work together."

"Just one?"

"That's all."

"Okay, thanks. I've done a first aid course." Olive hoped that would make him happy.

"And I'm assuming my mother looked at your references?"

"Oh, I've never done this before, but I've got a lot of younger cousins and several nieces and nephews. There are lots of children and babies in the community and we all do our fair share watching them."

Blake rolled his eyes and shook his head while his face turned an unflattering shade of red. "That woman… You mean you've got no references?"

Olive shook her head and wondered if she really would have to turn around and ride all the way home again. It had been a longer ride than she'd expected, too.

There was no more talk of references or Blake's mother as Blake quickly showed her the location of a bathroom, a couple of the spare bedrooms and Leo's room. "This is his upstairs bedroom. He has two. An upstairs one where he sleeps at night and the downstairs room where he naps during the day. He has everything he needs in both rooms."

Once they were back downstairs, Olive saw Leo on the floor playing with toy trucks. "Ollie, play now?"

Blake ignored his son, looked at his watch and then looked at Olive. "Coffee, I need coffee. Can you at least make coffee?"

Olive hesitated. Had he made up his mind already that he was not going to be satisfied with her performance? And, couldn't the man make his own coffee? "Yes, I can. Come with me, Leo; we can play later and now you can help me fix your daddy some coffee."

Leo jumped up and down and followed Olive into the kitchen. Minutes later, Blake appeared in the kitchen tying his tie.

"How do you have it?" Olive asked utterly distracted by a man getting dressed in front of her.

Blake sat on a stool behind the island countertop that separated them. "Just black, no sugar."

"That's easy." Olive placed the coffee in front of Blake then picked Leo up and balanced him on her hip. "He's only got underpants and socks on. I'll go and dress him."

Blake waved a large, tanned hand in the air. "Yes, then come right back so I can speak to you. I've got to leave soon."

"Oh, do you want me to cook you some breakfast?"

Blake shook his head. "No need. I always eat out." Olive nodded and made her way to Leo's bedroom.

"And don't let him talk you into playing before you come back," Blake called after them.

Olive looked into the little boy's face and whispered to him, "You've gotten us in trouble before breakfast." The boy laughed and buried his face into her shoulder as they made their way into Leo's downstairs bedroom.

The room was filled with toys and Olive considered that he could give two-thirds away to the poor and still have more toys than he would ever play with. "I've never seen so many toys except in a toy store." She set him down and dressed him for the day. She slipped a soft, yellow shirt over his head and snapped his overall clasps at his shoulders. She examined the stitches on the overalls and knew they must have cost a sum. The overalls were double-stitched and fully lined with a different fabric. *Humph, a far cry from Amish hand-me-downs.* As she tied his sneakers, Leo played with the strings of her prayer *kapp*.

"Hungry now, Ollie. Gimme some berries."

Olive laughed at how cute her name sounded when he tried to say it. "Leo, you should say, can I have some berries, please?"

"Can I have some berries, peeees?" Leo said with a sweet smile displaying his tiny white baby teeth.

"I will give you something, but let me finish here first. Then I'll see if you have berries in the fridge." Leo wound the strings of her prayer *kapp* around his fingers while she finished tying his left shoelace.

"I'm hungry, Ollie." Leo's voice raised.

She laughed at his demands and told him once more to say please. He did so, and then he jumped into her waiting arms.

Olive knew she would like playing with Leo every day; he was such a happy child and full of life. All she had to do now was prove to Blake she was the right person for the job. Refusing to hold her hand, Leo made his way down the stairs by himself, and then they headed to the kitchen. Olive settled the little boy into his special chair and set out to make breakfast for him.

Blake stopped her in her tracks. "What are you doing?" Olive was half in the refrigerator when he spoke to her.

She leaned back out with a bowl of strawberries in hand. "I'm making breakfast for Leo."

He stormed to the other side of the large, kitchen island and yanked a sheet of paper off the top. Blake shoved the paper in front of her. Olive tried to read what was on the paper, but he kept moving it.

"Blake, you're making me sick in the tummy moving the paper like that. What's on it?"

He huffed out a breath and slammed the paper down on the island. "It's the rules and instructions for the day. Including the fact berries give him a rash. It also states what breakfast is supposed to be." He ran a hand through his hair. "I don't think that this is a good idea. I don't think you're mature or experienced enough for this. Not that my mother cares at all what I think. I did also say that I wanted to speak with you. I assumed you would give me your full attention rather than start your duties before my mother arrives."

Leo ignored the tension in the room; all he wanted was berries. "Ollie, berries, pwease!"

Olive read the note to see that Leo had plain cereal for breakfast and nothing else. She prepared it and set it in front of him. Leo clapped in happiness at the sight of his food and Olive turned back to Blake. "You're quite right, Blake, I'm sorry, but I was distracted by Leo and I didn't think you'd keep anything in the fridge that didn't agree with him. He's quite capable of opening the door and reaching them if he really wanted to." Olive noticed Blake's face was red.

"What's the point? My mother's taken over my life once again. She was supposed to be here."

"Oh, that's nice. She's coming here?"

"She's supposed to be staying all day with you and Leo." He looked out the kitchen window where he could see the entrance of the driveway.

"She'll be with us all day?" Olive asked.

"Yes, I already told you that. I hope I won't have to tell you everything twice. I thought that it was best to ease Leo into things since he doesn't know you."

And neither did Blake know her, and Olive knew that was his real problem.

He glanced again at his watch. "I don't know what's keeping her. She knows I've got an important meeting and she's late. I'll call her." He reached into his pocket and pulled out his cell phone and pressed some buttons. A couple of seconds later, she answered. "Mother, where are you?"

"Hello, Blake. I'm on my way. Haven't you left yet?"

With her excellent hearing, Olive could hear the conversation.

"Remember our deal, Mother?" Blake glanced up at Olive, smiled and moved away. "Mother, how far away are you?"

"Not far. You go now and I'll be there soon…in a couple of minutes."

"Promise?"

"Of course. We made a deal."

Blake ended the call and shoved his phone back into his pocket, then swung around to face Olive.

"She's not far away and I have to go now. I've got a meeting to get to and I can't be late."

"We'll be fine."

"I hope so."

Chapter Five

Against his better judgement, Blake headed to his car and jumped in. The girl seemed harmless enough; even though she was a little vague, she did seem to care for Leo. When Blake was well clear of the house, he called his mother determined to deliver some stern words. What did she think she was doing saddling him with a mere girl, an Amish girl at that? How could this girl possibly be capable of looking after his son? And, where the hell was she? Finally, his mother answered the phone. "Mom, I hope you're not far away."

"Just a couple of minutes."

He sighed. "You said that a couple of minutes ago. Please hurry."

"I'm not far. Trust me."

He rolled his eyes. "Trust you? You didn't tell me she was Amish."

"I didn't think it relevant. If anything, it makes her more trustworthy. The Amish have big families and she's come from a large family; she told me so herself."

"You could have warned me, that's all. When I saw

her walk through the door I thought she was looking for converts."

Sonia laughed, and then quickly said, "I hope you weren't rude."

"Of course not." Blake ended the conversation and then turned his attention back to the road. What did he think he would achieve by speaking to his mother? She had never listened to him in the past. She thought she knew what was best for him and his life. If only she could be a proper grandmother, but she was too concerned with her social life to be bothered with boring things such as changing diapers. Maybe things would've been different if he'd had siblings, then her attention would have been more focused on her children and therefore her grandchildren.

That morning, he had hoped to turn the new nanny away politely and pay her for the trouble of coming there. But since she was there and Leo seemed pleased to see her, he had relented. When he'd watched how Olive thwarted one of Leo's tantrums, he thought she deserved a trial period. Now, he was annoyed with himself. It was just another win for his mother.

Leo needed more than a young nanny; he needed someone to guide him before his behavior became unmanageable. Blake knew his work kept him away too often to provide the structure Leo needed. *Olive's a pretty girl; it's a shame she's hidden away from the world living with the Amish. She's got a natural warmth and friendliness. I hope she did not take offence at my reaction to her. It's not her fault that she was swept up into my mother's scheming ways. I should apologize to the poor girl.*

* * *

Olive picked up Blake's list of instructions for Leo, sorting through what was important and what was not. There were far too many things on the list to remember by heart and Olive wanted to follow the most essential.

It was eleven o'clock when Olive heard a key jiggling in the lock of the front door. It opened to reveal Sonia.

"Hello, Sonia."

"Hello, how are you both getting along?"

"Nanna, Nanna." Leo ran to her with outstretched arms.

Sonia's face contorted as she took a step back. "Oh, you don't have dirty hands do you, Leo?"

Leo stopped still.

"Show me," she ordered.

Leo put up his hands, so his palms faced his grandmother. "Okay, now you can hug me." He wrapped his arms around her legs. "How are you, Olive?"

"Great. Leo and I are getting along fine."

"What about that son of mine?"

"Good. I think."

"Oh, don't concern yourself with him. He's just worried about Leo." She looked down at her grandson. "Go back and play with Olive. Nanna's going out to lunch." Sonia walked further into the room and Olive stood up from where she'd been playing with Leo.

"Blake said you were staying here for the whole day. For my entire first day."

"Just tell him I did." Sonia sat down on the couch.

Olive shook her head and sat next to her. "I can't do that. If he found out I wasn't telling him the truth he'd never trust me with Leo. Something tells me he's got a problem with trust."

"Well, you've got that right. I totally understand what you're saying. I won't make you lie for me."

Olive was relieved. "I feel like I'm squashed in the middle." Olive leaned forward and whispered, so Leo wouldn't hear, "Blake doesn't want me to look after Leo." The beep of the house phone ringing interrupted them. "Shall I get it?" Olive asked.

"Just let it go to message."

When the message kicked in, they both heard a woman's voice. "Blake, why aren't you taking my calls? Blake, Blake? Pick up. Since you're not answering your cell phone you must be home. Answer me!" The woman gave an angry grunt and then ended the call.

"You'll get used to that. Women chase my son ever since his wife…well, for quite some time. He has one woman he's interested in at the moment, but she's a cow. Blake knows how I feel about her."

"You said you're not staying all day?" A change of subject was sorely needed. Her boss's personal life was none of her business and neither did she want to hear about it.

"I've got a luncheon with friends. Blake will huff and puff, but then he'll calm down. I'll call him and clear it with him." She pulled out her cell phone and pressed a number. "Blake, everything's going fine. I've been here for hours. Don't have another panic attack." She hung up and looked over at Olive. "It went to message."

Sonia had lied and Olive hoped she wouldn't be questioned by Blake or it would come back on her somehow. "It's such a nice day that I thought Leo and I might take a walk to the park later. Would that be okay?"

"Yes. You've got the alarm codes of the house?"

"No. I don't."

"I'll show you how to set the alarm when you're going out and turn it back on when you come back."

"Oh, no, it's okay we'll stay here."

"No need. It's easy."

"I don't know."

"Olive, don't be so fearful. You only press some buttons and then lock the door. When you come home, you enter that same code. That's all."

"Thank you. Will it be okay with Blake for me to have the code?"

"Yes, staff normally have security codes. Don't worry so much, Olive. I'm sure my son tried to intimidate you. That's what he does to everyone. Don't be scared of him."

Olive nodded and when she saw Sonia glance at her diamond-encrusted wristwatch, she guessed Leo and she would soon be left alone. "Could you show me how to set the alarm now?"

"Sure. Follow me. I'll also show you what to do if you accidentally trigger the alarm."

Leo and Olive waved Sonia goodbye, and then Olive prepared peanut butter sandwiches and carrot sticks, and loaded them and some bottles of water into a small cooler she had found in the laundry room. She packed a small tote bag with a few toys and books, adding a small box of wet-wipes for cleaning their hands. Along with an oversized picnic blanket, Olive found a small ball and placed both in Leo's old stroller she had found in the garage. They were going outdoors into the fresh air, and the park just down the road was the perfect place. Leo insisted he wanted to walk, that he didn't want to get into the stroller. Olive decided that was a good idea;

she would set the cooler and the bag inside it rather than carry everything, and let Leo get the added exercise.

She tapped in the alarm code and heard the correct beeps, and then she locked the door behind them hoping she wouldn't accidently set off the alarm when they got back.

Once they finally reached the park after walking at toddler speed, Olive spread out the blanket and they ate under the warmth of the sun. After lunch, she pushed the little boy on the toddler swing and then chased him around the park until he exhausted himself. They sat down and Leo happily settled into her lap.

Olive pulled out one of his books and read aloud. After a while, Olive realized it didn't matter what the story was, it was all about the tone of her voice. Leo moved off her lap and laid down beside her. Olive kept on reading until his breathing slowed and he drifted off to sleep.

They stayed while Leo had a nap. Olive couldn't remember the last time she had felt this happy or this at peace. Her mind wandered as she felt Leo's warm breath fan across her skin. Her thoughts turned to Blake; he was a mystery to her. He seemed so angry, but why? She remembered the look on his face that morning as he watched her make the breakfast. It had broken her heart that he showed his anger in front of his young son.

Her eyes drifted to the little boy beside her. Leo looked so much like his dad except for the light hair. They were both so handsome, so… Olive shook that thought right out of her head. She had no business thinking about Blake being attractive. She was the nanny and Blake was in no way a suitable match for her, him being

an *Englischer* and all. Just in age alone… Blake must
have had over a decade on her.

A chilly wind started up, so Olive shut down all
thoughts of Blake and gathered their belongings. Once
everything was packed away, Olive picked up the
still sleeping boy into her arms and placed him in the
stroller. Even though he was too big for it, she was especially thankful she had brought it; she would never
have been able to carry him home. She covered Leo
with the blanket and quickly walked back to the house.

When they arrived home, Leo woke just as she'd
switched off the alarm. He helped her unload the
stroller, and they enjoyed the rest of the afternoon while
they waited for Blake's return. Olive felt a sense of sat-
isfaction that she had made it through the first day without any help from Sonia.

It was ten minutes past six when Olive heard Blake's
car in the driveway. She had no idea what hours she was
supposed to work and was glad that her mother had offered to keep her dinner aside for her. Leo and Olive
were playing with a train-set at one side of the living
room when Blake walked in the door of the room from
the adjoining garage.

Leo sprang to his feet. "Daddy, Daddy!" Blake
picked him up.

Olive stood up and smoothed down her dress. "Hello,
we've had a lovely day."

"Well, I haven't; I'm tired and I'm not in the best
of moods." He put Leo down, walked a few steps and
threw his keys down on a side-table. "My mother let
me down today. Look, I'm sorry about this morning.
I had no idea that my mother would employ a nanny."

"I'm sorry, I thought…"

"She said she could look after Leo herself. I told her it would be too much for her, but she had insisted. We had some conversations about a nanny, but you can understand my shock when she came here yesterday to tell me she'd hired a nanny. And today...don't even get me started on what she did to me today."

Olive scratched her neck. What did he want her to say? They had discussed all that earlier in the day. Whenever she got nervous, she broke out into a rash, and she did not like to have confrontations with people. "I understand it might frustrate you, but I'm here to help."

Blake nodded. "I appreciate it." He sat down on the couch and Leo climbed onto his lap. "What did you do today, Leo?"

"We wen to da park," Leo said.

"You did?" He looked over at Olive. "It's far too cold for the park in this weather."

"It was warm when we started out, and we came directly back when it began to turn cold. Before that though, we had a picnic, played on the swings and then Leo fell asleep."

"Fell asleep? He never has naps in the middle of the day. Miss Hesh, that simply won't do; you must try to keep him awake. Now, he won't go to sleep until past midnight. Neither of us will get any sleep. That was on the list—no naps. Didn't you read it? I handed it to you."

Her hand flew to her mouth. "I'm so sorry." She hadn't given one thought to his sleep routine and neither did she recall seeing it on the list.

"If I knew you wouldn't have read the list, I would not have bothered writing it. You can read, can't you?"

"Yes, I can read." She worked hard to contain her

reaction to the insult. "I'm so sorry; I was distracted. I read it through once, but just quickly."

His dark eyes seemed to bore through her. "A proper nanny would realize that you have to keep children to a strict routine."

Olive looked away. She couldn't disagree with what he said, but why did he have to speak so harshly?

"Has he had his bath, at least?" Blake's face was hard, like stone.

"Yes, he's had his dinner and his bath."

As Blake looked back at Leo, he said, "That's something, I suppose."

Olive was annoyed with herself. He'd given her the list, why hadn't she taken more notice of it? "I'll take the instructions home and read them through."

"Home? You mean you're not live-in?"

"No; your mother said nothing about being live-in." Olive frowned; she was not sure how the bishop would react to her living in the house of a single *Englisch* man. *Nee*, it would not be approved of. "I can't do that; I'm sorry."

"I assumed you would, I mean that's what a nanny does, I thought. Anyway, it's late, how will you get home?"

"I've got my bike outside."

He looked her up and down. "Amish may ride bikes but not drive cars?"

Olive nodded. "It's a pedal bike. No motor. What time do you want me to start and finish each day? That is, if you still want me to work here."

Blake scratched his head. "I'm prepared to give it the one week, as we agreed this morning, and see how things go. Be here by eight. I vary the times I finish, so can you be here until I come home?"

Olive nodded again. "Yes, I can do that." Leo gave a big yawn. "Looks like you might get some sleep," Olive said, smiling at Leo's tired face.

Blake looked down at his son. "He does look a little sleepy."

"Good night, Leo. I'll see you tomorrow." Leo looked up at her and smiled sweetly. "Good night, Blake."

"I hope I didn't make things too difficult for you. My mother keeps telling me my temper is getting worse. I couldn't believe she didn't stay the day, like she said she would. Thank you for today, Olive."

Olive tingled inside on hearing Blake say her name. "Not at all," she said speaking in the most businesslike tone she could muster.

"I also must apologize again for my reaction to you being Amish. It was just that I thought my mother would have told me."

"She most likely considered that it wasn't a factor as it wouldn't affect my looking after Leo."

Blake frowned a little and avoided eye contact with Olive. "Yes, that would be it."

Olive left the house and walked to her bike, relieved to be getting away from Blake and his temper. She reminded herself that it was just the first day, and it was natural that it would be a difficult one. Her mother had taught her to look at the other person's point of view in every situation. As she rode her bike down the street, she considered things from Blake's point of view. He was a grown man, and forced by his mother into having a nanny and it wasn't even a nanny he had chosen. No wonder he was cranky, especially after Sonia tell-

ing him she'd stay the whole day, when clearly, she'd
never had any intention of doing so.

Blake felt bad over the way he'd treated Olive just
now. He knew she hadn't been expecting to be a live-in
nanny. He was just trying to make her feel more inad-
equate than he knew she already felt. Lashing out like
that was a flaw that he knew he had, born out of frustration. He looked at his watch. A security firm techni-
cian was coming any minute to install cameras in and
around the house. Then he'd be able to observe Olive
and Leo from his computer or his iPhone at any given
moment of the day. With his mother out of the picture,
this option would give him peace of mind.

From Olive's demeanor, he knew she was doing her
best. He also knew the Amish had a reputation of being
trustworthy people and loving children, and that must
have been why his mother felt confident in choosing her
for a nanny. If he'd had his way, he would have gotten
someone both reliable and experienced, but he seldom
had his way with his mother around.

He'd have to make up for his bad temper and make
Olive feel more welcome. Maybe she would work out
and be an answer to his problems. After he had poured
himself a drink and sat down on the couch, he continued
to mull over the situation. Would he ever stop worrying
about Leo? He'd worried about Leo every day when he
was with his grandmother, and now he had a nanny and
he was still worried about him.

Blake slowly savored his first sip of gin and tonic,
took a deep breath and let it out slowly, and tried to let
his body relax. He decided that no matter if the best
trained nanny in the world were looking after his son,

he'd still find reason to worry. He glanced at his wrist-watch again.

The security people were late.

The next morning, with his new camera system raising his confidence about Olive looking after Leo, Blake was determined to be a much nicer person. He put the coffee machine on just before Olive was due to arrive. Perhaps if they sat down and had a talk over a cup of coffee they could get to know one another better and that way she might understand that his abrupt manner was partly from his personality and partly derived from stress.

Leo was busy playing in the living room when Olive knocked on the door. Blake turned around and said to Leo, "I'll bet that's Olive."

Leo turned his head and looked upward.

"Olive's at the door. Do you want to come and see?" Leo was off running to the door.

"Don't run too fast." Blake's warning fell on deaf ears as always. He managed to get there before Leo and after he scooped Leo up in his arms, he opened the door and fixed a smile on his face. He was determined to be nice to Olive today and show her he wasn't the ogre he'd seemed the day before.

The young woman's face broke out into a delighted grin when she saw Leo with his outstretched arms.

"Good morning, Leo."

"What do you say, Leo?" his father asked him. "You say, 'Good morning, Miss Olive.'"

"Good morning, Miss Oliff."

"G'morning, Leo, Blake," Olive said as she stepped in through the doorway.

Blake put Leo down on the floor and Leo hurried to stand by Olive.

"I just made a pot of coffee; would you like some?"

He noticed that Olive appeared reluctant, and then she said, "Yes, that would be nice, thank you."

"I thought we could have a quick talk about things over coffee." He looked down at Leo. "Go back and play with your toys for a minute. Daddy wants to talk to Miss Olive."

"I want to play." He grasped a handful of Olive's skirt and attempted to pull her into the living room.

"I'll come soon, Leo, but first I have to talk to your dad."

"I don't think he'll go play by himself now with you here."

"Should I bring some toys in, so he can sit by us while we talk?" Olive asked.

"That sounds like a good idea."

"I'll fetch some. Do you want to come with me, Leo?"

"Yes."

Olive took hold of Leo's hand and headed to the living room to choose a few toys. Her heart pounded wondering what Blake wanted to talk to her about. He was smiling, so she guessed he wasn't going to terminate her employment just yet. Perhaps he was simply going tell her some guidelines, but then again, he had his list of those. When she gathered up some toys and Leo had a toy truck in each hand, they headed back to the kitchen.

"Here's your coffee. How do you have it?"

"Just black is fine, thank you."

"Really?" He pulled a face, even though he usually drank his the same way.

"I don't have it black all the time. Sometimes I have a latte with caramel in it if I go to a café." Olive giggled nervously when she realized what she'd just said. "I mean, a latte with caramel in it." After she had put Leo's toys on the floor and he was occupied, she took her seat up at the countertop opposite Blake. "Can I make you some breakfast?"

He shook his head. "I have breakfast at a café while I'm reading the newspaper. I like to know what's going on in the world before I start my day." He took a mouthful of coffee. "I suppose it's irrelevant to you what's going on in the world?"

"Only if it affects me. Otherwise, I don't care about celebrities changing their hairstyles."

Blake gave a low chuckle. "Is that what you think's in the newspapers?"

"That's what I see in the magazines at the coffee shop."

"That's very different from what's in the newspaper."

"I've seen they write about what celebrity is marrying or divorcing in the newspapers. I suppose there's news on politics and crimes; are you talking about things of that nature?"

"You could say that."

"Then you're right, things like that don't interest me." She hoped that answer was okay because she wasn't there to tutor Leo, just to look after him. She remained silent waiting for Blake to speak.

"I want to apologize for being harsh to you yesterday. I was rude and said a few things that I wished I could take back."

"You apologized yesterday, and that's fine. Everyone has a hard day now and again. Or an off-day."

He slowly nodded. "That's very generous of you, but I just wanted to let you know that I'm not nasty, I just want what's best for my son."

"I totally understand. Children are the most important things… Oh, I don't mean that children are things." She giggled, and then cleared her throat. "Let me try that again; I know if I had a child, that child would be everything to me."

He nodded again. "Leo is everything to me." He studied her for a moment. "I'm glad you understand."

"I do. I'll look after Leo very well."

"I've got no doubt you will. I just wanted to say I'm sorry." He took another mouthful of coffee. "More than say I'm sorry. I just wanted to let you know that I'm not a horrible person."

She nodded. "That's fine."

He drained the last of his coffee and stared into the mug. "Leo needs to eat. He hasn't had his breakfast yet and the list of instructions is on the fridge where it always is."

She nodded. "Okay."

Blake couldn't stop himself from giving her more instructions even though he had told her everything the day before. He got in his car, opened the automatic garage door and backed out of the garage. As he made his way down the drive, he considered Olive. She was quite unlike any woman he had ever met. She was so sweet and she clearly loved children. If only the women he usually dated had those qualities. All they cared about was looking good and wearing the latest fashions. He'd only begun to date again in the last few months and so far he'd found no one he could see himself with; certainly, no one he'd let become close to Leo. He stopped the car and pulled out his iPhone and opened the app so he could observe the new nanny. She was wiping down the kitchen countertops and was talking to Leo as he ate his cereal. He had no sound on the app, but he didn't need sound to make sure his son was okay. Satisfied Leo was safe for now, he continued down the driveway.

Blake's mind drifted to the kind of women he'd been dating. Perhaps he'd been looking for companionship in the wrong places. If he went back to church, he might meet a different kind of woman; a woman kind and gentle, just like Olive except older. Yes, he could see himself fully committing to a woman like that.

Olive was relieved that he had apologized—again— for his behavior. She could understand it. With no mother around it was only natural he would be worried about Leo while he was at work. She had been blessed with a mother and a father and many siblings, but poor little Leo only had a father, and with his father's unfortunate personality there was little chance Leo would have siblings anytime soon.

It became a habit of Blake's to look on his phone every spare minute of the day to check on his son. All he saw was his son lovingly cared for and, when need be, "guided" rather than punished when he'd done something wrong. He'd never admit it to her face, but his mother had done a fantastic job of finding Olive. All the same, he had to keep Olive on her toes. He knew if he gave any of his employees an inch, they'd take a mile and this nanny, as nice as she was, would undoubtedly be no different.

Chapter Six

A few days along, Olive thought Blake would've gotten used to her looking after Leo. He had apologized for his rudeness several times, but he hadn't changed his attitude.

Every morning followed the same routine; Blake greeted her with a list of things from the day before that she could've or should've done better. She did not understand why he was so hard on her. Blake always found some reason to complain. After another early morning reprimand, she heard the screeching tires of his car as it sped away. Sometimes Blake was so frustrating, she wanted to shout at him, but she loved looking after Leo and appreciated the wages.

She had walked up to Leo's upstairs bedroom, tears welling in her eyes, to get Leo out of his pajamas and change him into his day clothes, when she heard a key jiggling in the front door.

"Olive, it's me. I need to talk to you, dear." It was Sonia Worthington. Sonia had called in nearly every day to see how she was getting along with Blake, and

Olive had found out she was not the only one who thought Blake was hard to get along with.

"I'm just dressing Leo; I'll be right there." Olive tried her best to control her shaking voice. She wiped her tears and checked herself in the mirror; Mrs. Worthington should not see she had been crying. She came downstairs with Leo to see Sonia sitting at the kitchen table.

"Come here, my dear, sit down with me," Mrs. Worthington said.

"Nana, Nana," Leo shouted as he ran toward his grandmother, and then climbed on her lap.

"What is it you wanted to talk about, Mrs. Worthington. Sorry, I mean, Sonia?" Olive took a seat.

"Oh, nothing so important, dear. Tell me, how are you doing? Have you settled in well? Are things getting any easier?"

Olive studied Sonia and wondered how Blake could be her son considering how nice and polite she was. *I rarely see a glimpse of her in him. I know that deep down he might be nice too, but I can't comprehend why he's so rude and aggressive toward me.* "I'm fine, Sonia. Thank you for asking. I'm fine, nothing's wrong. I like it here."

"I just called in to apologize, my dear," Sonia said.

"Apologize for what?"

"I know it's already tough for you to come here and work for a man who's ungrateful. I've heard the way he speaks to you. I'm afraid what happened with his wife was very hard on him. I doubt he'll ever recover. The wounds are too deep. There are some things in life from which one simply can't recover."

Olive nodded, knowing it would be hard to lose a loved one. Her *grossmammi* and *grossdaddi* were still alive on both sides of the family, but she knew that one day she'd lose someone close and that would be painful.

Sonia continued, "Please forgive him; he's become aggressive toward everyone. I've given it some thought; I think he gets upset when he sees you taking care of Leo so well. It reminds him of her, and he lashes out in frustration."

"That makes sense. I appreciate you telling me this, Sonia. I thought he scolded me because I wasn't doing my job properly, seeing as I've no experience or training. I know I do have trouble concentrating. My head's in the clouds, my mother always tells me."

Sonia leaned forward. "I'm afraid you aren't in a winning position. No matter how well you look after Leo, Blake will never be happy. It'll just remind him of Mona, his late wife. He'll most likely come around in time, but please don't leave over his bad moods. Leo needs you."

"Thank you, that makes things easier for me. My mother often tells me to look at the other person's point of view. *There are two sides to everything and we only know our side,* she says all the time."

"Your mother's a wise woman."

Olive would not normally ask questions, but since Sonia offered information she was curious to know more. "Did his wife die a long time ago?"

"Just about a year ago."

"Oh, that's so sad. And, he's not met another woman since? I mean he is rich and handsome." Olive knew that comfort and wealth were important to *Englischers*, as well as outer beauty.

"Sounds like you have a crush on my son." Sonia raised an eyebrow.

Olive put her hand to her mouth as she giggled. "It's nothing like that. I mean, anyone would find him attractive. He's a handsome man, but I was just making an observation." Sonia continued to look at her, which caused Olive to add, "He wouldn't suit me since he's not an Amish man."

Sonia tossed her head back and laughed.

Olive felt heat rise in her cheeks. Sonia hadn't been serious and here she was explaining herself. Sonia would know she could not consider a relationship with an *Englischer*. "I feel silly. I have a habit of blurting things out."

"Come on now, Olive, don't try to fool an old lady. I'm much older than I look. My natural hair color is white and, thanks to various technologies, my wrinkles are kept at bay. I didn't get to be this age without learning a thing or two about love." Sonia shook her head. "All women fall in love with my son and, the annoying thing is, he knows it. He could have any woman he wants. I'm sure of it. Leo will be just the same. He has that same determined streak along with the looks." Sonia stared at Olive. "Blake would do well to find a nice woman like you; that's what he needs."

"No, it's not like that really. He was a little nice the morning after the first day and from then on, he's not been nice. Oh, I'm not complaining, just trying to point out that I couldn't possibly have a crush on someone like that. No offense, or anything, since he's your son."

"That simply won't do. I'll talk with him. He's got no right to be rude after you've been so good to work for us."

Olive gasped. She didn't want to make trouble. "Please don't do that. Things will work themselves out

I'm sure. If you were right about him being upset about his wife he needs to work things out in his own time."

"Very well, but if it continues for much longer you must let me know."

"I will," Olive said. "It's only natural he'd take a long time to get over his wife's death."

"Life can throw some strange things our way, but we have to keep moving."

Olive nodded thinking of the Scripture that the rain falls on the just and the unjust alike. Bad things happen to good people.

"Just remember, dear, let me know if you need anything. You already take such good care of Leo. I'm sure you'll eventually smooth things out with Blake too." Sonia patted Olive's hand. "I've some errands to run today. I'll call by again this afternoon and spend some time with Leo."

"Yes, Leo would love that." Olive and Leo said goodbye to Sonia and closed the door. *Blake must have some good in him since his mother's so lovely*, Olive thought as she walked up the stairs with Leo.

Driving like a reckless teenager, putting one hand on the horn and increasing his speed, Blake thought back to what happened at the breakfast table that first day. He'd written the note telling Olive not to feed Leo berries, and she hadn't taken time to read it. She was a risk to his son's health. A properly trained and qualified nanny would have a way of remembering something as important as allergies. Then she tried to make him feel it was his fault. He couldn't allow her to endanger her son's health, no matter how attractive and pleasant Olive was.

Olive goes along thinking she can do as she pleases just because she's the only one who can make Leo behave. She has to learn things have consequences. Maybe she doesn't realize the importance of her position as Leo's nanny. Mother doesn't understand what kind of people are in the world. Just because Olive's Amish doesn't mean she's perfect. I need to find someone who can look after Leo properly. Despite what my mother thinks, a mere girl can't be expected to take on the responsibility of Leo for any length of time.

Blake's bad mood wasn't helped when the lights of a police car flashed in his rearview mirror. He pulled over and sat seeking patience with the engine turned off. He pulled out his driver's license and the registration papers for his car. After a few moments, the police officer got out of his car and sauntered toward him. Blake smiled at him when he reached his window. "Was I speeding, officer?"

"License and registration." He took Blake's license and papers from him. "You were over the speed limit."

"I'm sorry, I've got a problem at home. A new nanny and I'm worried about my son."

The officer looked at the name on the license. "Are you the Worthington from Worthington Industries?"

Blake smiled. The man recognized him, which meant he'd let him off. "Yes, I am."

The officer's lips turned down, and he slowly shook his head. "People like you always think you're above the law."

"Now hang on a minute, I'm under a great deal of stress."

"Stress? They're not renewing your country club membership?"

Blake clutched the steering wheel and looked ahead. Then the officer proceeded to walk around the car, and Blake knew he was looking for something else he could cite him for. Blake called out, "There's nothing wrong with the car. I had new tires put on only last week, and it's also been serviced. It's barely a year old."

The officer walked back to the window. "New tires and it's less than a year old? What sort of driving do you do?"

Blake scratched his cheek. "I just wanted different ones."

"Ah, the factory fitted ones not good enough, eh?" The officer shook his head.

From his comments, it seemed the officer was struggling to make ends meet. He probably had two ex-wives to support and lived in a ramshackle house in a bad neighborhood. It was clear he hated people with wealth. Blake stayed quiet fearing he'd enrage the officer further.

"Stay there; we're not done yet." The officer took another look around the car.

Blake was considering slipping him a couple of hundred-dollar bills to forget the whole thing. Then again, that could get him into even more trouble seeing as the officer had a grudge against him.

After what seemed an eternity later, the officer reappeared, handed him a ticket and returned his license and registration papers. "Watch your speed," he snarled. "You're just as accountable as the rest of us."

Blake gave a polite nod as he put away his license and registration, and then he took hold of the ticket. Without looking at the dollar amount of the fine, he shoved the ticket in his glove box. He'd have one of his personal assistants look after it tomorrow.

This could be a sign that I have to do something about that woman. Enough is enough; I need to talk to Mom. Maybe she can find Olive a job somewhere with one of her friends. I know Mom will have every excuse under the sun to keep Olive on, but it makes no sense. Leo needs a proper nanny to look after him. He pulled away from the curb making sure he signaled, and drove at a moderate speed. A couple of miles down the road, his phone rang on the Bluetooth connection. "Hello."

"Blake, it's me."

He recognized the voice of Jo, a woman he'd dated infrequently over the last weeks. "Hello, I've been meaning to call you."

"I heard you got a nanny."

"That's right. How did you know?"

"I called the house."

If he wasn't upset before, he was definitely upset now. "You spoke to the nanny?"

"No, your mother."

"I see." He was at least pleased his mother had been at the house.

"Anyway, I'm back and now we'll be able to see a lot more of one another."

Had she gone somewhere? He hadn't noticed. "Okay."

"You don't sound very pleased about it. Have I called at a bad time?"

"I'm sorry, I'm just distracted. I just got a speeding ticket."

"Oh, I'm sorry."

"It's a bad start to the day."

"How about we go out for dinner tonight to cheer you up?"

She was trying hard. He wasn't really that keen, but she wasn't a bad kind of person. "Tonight would be too short notice, and I don't have anyone to look after Leo."

"What about the nanny?"

He sighed. What he probably needed was a day nanny and a night nanny. "She's a day nanny."

"You might have to get a nighttime nanny."

"Hmm. I was just thinking that. I could see if she could stay late one night."

"You could?"

Blake knew he had to get on with his life, and he hoped to marry again so Leo wouldn't be an only child. He wanted Leo to have two parents and not feel different from his peers. To achieve that, he had to date, and Jo was okay. She might be a good choice. "I'll ask if she can stay tomorrow night for a bit longer, how's that?"

"Thanks."

"I'll call you tonight. I've got another call coming in."

"Okay. Bye, Blake."

With a flick of a finger, he ended the call. He didn't really have another call coming in; he didn't like to chitchat on the phone about nothing and that was what Jo was prone to do.

Later that day, Sonia came back to the house to see Leo as promised. Sonia entertained Leo in his playroom while Olive cleaned up.

"I'll wash some of Leo's clothes; his laundry basket is full." Olive carried the basket downstairs and into the laundry. She'd already noticed there was a large electric washer and clothes dryer in there and she was keen to try them out. At her *haus*, she had no clothes dryer at all and in the wet weather they hung their clothes on a line in the barn. Their washing machine was gas-powered and nowhere near the size of the one in Blake's house. With appliances like Blake's the washing could be done at any time of the day, not just in the morning.

"Do you need any help, Olive?" Sonia called out, "I told you that we have people to clean once a week and that includes the weekly washing."

"No, I'm almost done in the laundry."

"Then when you're done can you bathe Leo? He's just drawn all over himself with marker-pens and Blake will be furious if he sees him like this. I would help but I don't want to risk getting my dress wet."

"I'll be right there." Olive hurried upstairs and gave Leo his bath. Just as she had him dry and dressed in his pajamas, Olive heard a door opening downstairs.

Sonia, who had joined them in Leo's bedroom, said, "That must be Blake."

Olive glanced across at Sonia, and they shared a knowing look.

Leo heard his father downstairs. "Daddy, Daddy." He bolted to the top of the stairs.

Olive held his hand and helped him down, even though he was quite capable of doing it himself; Sonia followed along behind them.

When Blake scooped up Leo into his arms, Sonia asked, "Blake, how was your day?"

"Not good. Amongst other annoying things, I got a speeding ticket."

"You shouldn't have been driving too fast. Be careful next time," his mother said.

Blake frowned and sat down on the couch. "Can you get me a glass of water, Olive?"

"Sure." Olive walked into the kitchen, opened a bottle of cold water, poured it into a glass and just as she was about to walk back into the living room, she heard her name mentioned.

"I want to talk to you about Olive," Blake said.

"Yes?" she heard Sonia say.

"I've been giving her a lot of thought and we don't know anything about this girl. She also isn't from our world. I've got nothing against her but we know nothing about her except the few things she's told us. How can we have hired some stranger to look after my son?"

"I'm confident she's the right person for the job. Qualifications aren't everything. You just need to think positively. In fact, you need to be more positive in general. You're always looking at the downside of everything. She's no longer a stranger, and she's doing splendidly. Have you seen any bad behavior from the cameras around the house?"

Cameras? thought Olive. *What on earth…*

"Well, no."

Their conversation ended when Olive came back into the room with the water. "Blake, would you like me to make you some dinner, or have you eaten out again?"

"I could do with a salad. That's all I feel like."

Olive nodded. "I'll fix you one." She hurried back to the kitchen horrified that he had cameras on her. Could he see her while he was at work? It certainly sounded that way.

"Leo is happy with her and she's treating him as her own son," Sonia said.

Olive was certain they had a few more things to say

about her but decided not to listen. Whatever Blake thought of her was something she could do nothing about. *If* Gott *wants me to work here, then things will work out, and if not, then* Gott *will place me somewhere else,* Olive thought.

When his mother finally left, Blake told Olive he had a special request.

"I have an appointment tomorrow night, and I wondered if you'd be able to stay a little later?"

She nodded. "That should be okay."

"Normally I wouldn't ask, but I'm confident with you looking after him and I don't want to ask my mother. I don't trust anyone else with Leo."

Finally, he trusted her. Olive was so pleased to hear it. *So, if that's true, what is going on with the cameras?*

"I can drive you home afterward. I wouldn't want you driving home late on your bike."

Olive gave a little giggle. "What's funny?"

"Riding home on my bike, not driving."

Blake smiled. "Riding then."

"That would be no good. Leo would have to be dragged out of bed for you to take me home."

"That's true. You could stay the night here if you wish."

Olive shook her head; even if she were okay with it, her parents would never allow that, especially since he was a single man. "I'd be happy to stay later, but I can't do overnight."

"Good enough. You'll be paid properly for overtime."

Olive nodded slightly. She didn't like talking about money although she liked receiving it.

"As I said, it's a pesky work thing, but every now and again I have to attend these things."

"I understand."

When Olive was gone, Blake had no idea why he just hadn't come straight out and told her he had a date. What did he care what she thought? It was then that he faced the truth; he was attracted to her. It made no sense. She would think him far too old and cranky. Besides that, she was Amish.

He ran a hand through his dark hair. If only he'd met someone like Olive years ago his life might've turned out differently. All he could do was wait for time to pass and the pieces of his life to merge back together. Now, he was grateful Olive was Leo's nanny for however long she could stay in his employment.

Chapter Seven

Olive made it a point to arrive early the next morning. She found Blake drinking coffee while watching Leo draw on a large pad on the kitchen table. They both turned to look at her when she walked in.

She saw a pile of clothes, and it appeared Blake had attempted to dress his son at some point. Blake didn't bat an eye as he pushed the small pile of clothes toward Olive. "I give up; you dress him." He continued to sip his coffee.

Olive had no trouble dressing Leo and not long after that, Blake left for work.

She cleaned up the breakfast dishes and searched the kitchen for the daily list, but there was none. "Well, well, well. I don't believe it!" Olive stood in the middle of the kitchen shocked. Blake had conceded a tiny bit of control.

Leo often wore more food than he ate and today was no different. Olive took him upstairs and changed his clothes for the second time. When they were back in the living room, they settled into a serious building competition with Leo's wooden blocks. They were in the middle of it when someone came through the front door. In a panic, Olive quickly shielded Leo until she saw who it was. She let out a relieved breath when it was just Blake's mother.

Sonia glanced across at Olive and said, "I was hoping to find you two at home."

"Nana, Nana!" Leo yelled and clapped in glee as he struggled to get out of Olive's hold.

Olive watched the toddler leap into his grandmother's arms before she left the two of them alone.

The beautifully groomed woman followed Olive into the kitchen and sat down observing Olive. "So my dear, how are you doing with my boys?" The smile on her face hinted of mischief.

Olive tried to laugh but faltered. "I think that I'm doing okay. I don't think Blake's entirely happy with me, but we're still getting to know each other." She giggled to cover her nerves. "Things are improving. He didn't leave me a list this morning."

Sonia watched her a bit longer then rose to her feet. "Good, and I think we should get to know each other better too. I have an idea for the afternoon." She clapped her hands. "There's a cartoon-character ice-skating show at the arena today; I think we should treat our boy to a fun afternoon. Let's go; we have fun awaiting us." Sonia's enthusiasm was contagious, and soon Olive was preparing snacks and a drink for Leo.

They piled into Sonia's luxury sedan and headed off for an afternoon full of surprises. Olive was equally curious and nervous about what the day would reveal, but she genuinely liked Blake's mother.

When they arrived at the arena, Olive said, "Sonia, I won't be comfortable going in. I'll stay in the car."

"You can't go in?"

Olive shrugged. "Most likely, it's better if I don't."

"I understand. I think the show goes for an hour or more. Will you be all right here in the car?"

"*Jah*, of course. I'll just wait here. I'm happy to do that."

Olive sat and watched the little boy pull hard on Sonia's arm, eager to get to his destination. Over an hour later, grandmother and grandson returned. Sonia looked exhausted, and even Leo looked tired. Olive strapped Leo in his seat and wrapped a blanket around him to fight off the chill.

"How was the show, Sonia?"

"The skaters went onto the ice and the kids in the arena cheered and laughed. Leo had so much fun." Sonia leaned in, and whispered to Olive, "He's so much like his father you know. They are so happy and full of life." At Olive's disbelieving look, she laughed. "No, I'm serious. Blake was so full of life, so excited, but that all ended with the Mona situation." Olive knew heartache could change a person. Glancing around, she saw that Leo had already fallen asleep. "Will you tell me what happened, Sonia? I don't want to pry, but he seems so angry now. It can't be good for a person to hold all that inside."

Sonia's eyes watered as she nodded her head. She stared off into the parking lot and turned on the ignition. "They were high school sweethearts. Blake spent years building a name for himself in the business world before he proposed, and then a second later, they were pregnant."

Sonia's car joined the line leaving the parking lot.

Olive wondered whether Sonia missed Leo's mother. Could they have been close?

"Mona was demanding and impossible throughout the pregnancy. She did not understand that Blake had to work to pay for her increasingly more expensive lifestyle."

Ah, that answers that question.

That was all Sonia said and Olive did not want to pry further about the matter.

"Are you able to eat lunch with us at a bistro?" Sonia asked.

"Yes, I eat out often. My friends and I go to the same coffee shop nearly every week." Olive missed her friends; she had seen little of them lately. She looked at Leo again. "He's asleep. I suppose I could hold him while we eat."

"No. We'll wake him. Blake doesn't like him to sleep too much during the day."

When they were parked at their destination, Sonia shook Leo's shoulder and he woke up immediately and looked around. "We're getting some food now. Come with us."

They found a table out in the garden area. The women ordered their lunch and enjoyed Leo's silliness as he raced around with other toddlers in the play area.

The afternoon would have been perfect except Olive could not stop thinking about Blake and Mona. He'd lost so much, it was no wonder he was angry all the time. Olive tried to imagine a happy and carefree version of Blake. The only version of him she could envision was the uptight, grumpy businessman who greeted her every day.

Leo exhausted himself and during the drive back to the house he fell asleep once again.

Once Sonia left, Olive cooked the dinner. With Leo having settled himself on the couch for another sleep, she concentrated on preparing a meal.

When Blake came home, he told Olive he wanted a word with her. She hoped it wasn't to reprimand her about Leo sleeping so much. She really couldn't help it if he had fallen asleep. It wasn't as though she'd put him to bed, and he'd been far too tired for distractions to keep him awake and happy.

He took a slow deep breath, then said, "I'm going on a date. It's not a work function."

"Oh. I see." She wondered why he was telling her this.

"I don't know why I lied."

"It's okay. I don't need to know where you're going."

"I know that!" His dark eyes blazed.

Olive was taken aback, and kept silent.

He shook his head. "I'm sorry. I'm under a lot of pressure and I shouldn't take it out on you."

"It's okay."

"It's not okay. Not in the least." He stood up and pushed the stool back under the kitchen island countertop. "I'll be leaving in half an hour and it won't be a late night."

"Take your time."

He gave her a nod and strode out of the room.

Once Blake had left for his date and she was bathing Leo, Olive couldn't help thinking what it would be like to have Blake's full attention. If he liked a woman, surely he'd talk sweetly to her. She found herself wanting him to like her as a woman. Pangs of envy toward the woman he was dating niggled at her.

On the way to the restaurant, Blake knew he couldn't go through with it. He pulled to the side of the road, parked his car and called his "date." He told her Leo had come down with a cold and he wouldn't be able to make it. She hung up in his ear. Apparently, his lie hadn't been convincing.

There was no point in going to see some other woman when the one he wanted to spend time with was the same young woman who was under his own roof at this very moment.

If Olive was ever going to have feelings for him, though, he'd have to rid himself of the chip on his shoulder. He knew that. Even though they were from two different worlds, he could see himself with a woman like Olive.

Just as Olive was done preparing Leo's food, she heard the garage door open. She walked to the internal door and was met by Blake. "You're so early. I have only just put Leo's meal out for him."

"She couldn't make it after all."

"Oh, I'm sorry about that."

He pulled an odd little smile. "I'm not." She stared at him not sure what he meant.

"When he finishes eating, we'll get you home."

"Okay." She gathered up her things, a little disappointed he hadn't suggested they have a cup of coffee. It would've been nice to have a quiet moment with him during the time Leo was occupied with eating. Who was she kidding? She was just the nanny.

"Ready?" he asked when he'd wiped Leo's hands.

"Yes."

"Come on, Leo. We're going to drive Miss Olive home." Leo held onto his father's outstretched hand.

Olive followed them through the house to the garage. There wasn't much conversation on the way home, and Olive had to wonder why he hadn't been more upset his date had canceled. When things didn't go his way, he normally got upset.

Chapter Eight

Two weeks later, Olive needed time with her four close friends. She organized them to meet at "their" coffee shop on Saturday morning. After Blake's failed date with that woman, she had admitted to herself that she found him appealing, but she wasn't ready to admit it to her friends.

Olive was pleased when one of her older brothers, Elijah, offered to drive her into town and come fetch her two hours later. Her legs ached from the constant bike riding over the past weeks to and from Blake and Leo's house, although she had noticed her muscles were getting stronger and she didn't tire as easily.

When Elijah asked about her new job, she told him she enjoyed it and loved looking after the little boy. She didn't tell him how she felt nothing she did for her boss was good enough. Blake had been less tough on her as time went by. And, there'd never been any more talk about that one week trial period, so he must've been mostly satisfied with her.

The drive to the coffee shop was just enough time for her to plan what she would tell her friends. Olive knew from experience they'd be relentless in asking questions to extract every detail of her new job. She'd seen them all at the Sunday meeting, but this was the first time in ages they'd be sitting down and talking together, just the five of them.

When she arrived, she was surprised they were all on time. Not only that, they were sitting and waiting for her at their regular table. Soon, tall steaming cups spread across the table along with a variety of pastries. Oftentimes on their outings, each would order a different pastry or cake and each girl would have a taste of every one.

"For someone who's just landed a well-paid job as a nanny you don't look very happy." Jessie's eyes bored through Olive's thin disguise of a smile.

Of all her friends, Jessie would be the one to notice that something was not right.

Jessie watched her from across the table waiting for Olive to speak, but Amy spoke first. "*Nee*, you don't, Olive."

The girls all leaned in, waiting for her response. She was tempted to shrug off their concerns and tell them everything was fine, but they knew her too well to do that. "Some things about the job are great. I love looking after Leo. The house is amazing, and Leo's grandmother is extremely nice."

"Then what's the problem?" one of the girls asked.

"Leo's father is a different kind of a man. He makes me feel awkward." So they wouldn't guess she liked him a little too much, she added, "He's a little grumpy. I'm trying not to take it personally."

"Why's he grumpy?" Claire asked.

"Mrs. Worthington, his mother, told me her son is

angry all the time because he's deeply hurt." Olive lowered her voice. "His wife died about a year ago, and now it seems that he's cranky with the whole world, but it lands on me." Her friends exchanged looks but said nothing. "You don't understand; his mother said he was different before that. He was full of life and so much fun. Now, he's not happy about anything and… he's taking it out on me." That wasn't entirely true, and Olive wasn't quite sure why she'd added that last piece of information.

"Why would he take it out on you?" Jessie asked.

"That day at the farmers market, Blake's mother gave me the job outright. I guess Blake's mad with her for doing that and he can't take it out on her, his own mother." Olive shrugged.

Claire leaned forward and held Olive's hand. "Um, Olive, can I ask you a question? What does Blake look like?" The other girls turned to her and snickered while waiting for her to answer.

Olive thought about it and felt that the truth would not hurt. "He's attractive in an older-man sort of way. I can see how women might find him interesting. His mother says all women fall in love with him, and he could have any woman he wants." Olive pulled her hand away from Claire's.

Claire leaned back into her seat and slapped a hand over her mouth, stifling laughter that appeared to be bubbling. Amy playfully slapped Claire's arm and tried to remain serious.

It was the forthright Jessie, who said, "So you think he's handsome, and you absolutely love his son; that's interesting."

Olive couldn't believe what she heard. That was not

what she meant them to hear; he was just her employer and she ought to have no other feelings for him except empathy for his situation.

Amy interrupted Olive's thoughts just in time. "We get it, Olive, I mean, it's not hard to fall in love with someone, but be careful. It's not fun to be delusional, but feel free to come to any of us if you need someone to talk to."

They all dissolved into laughter at the way Amy spoke, and Olive couldn't help laughing with them. When they were through with laughing, they told Olive about each of their job situations.

The stall at the farmers market had been successful for most of them. Jessie Miller found a position as a housekeeper, Amy Yoder obtained a position looking after an *Englisch* lady's children after school, Saturdays and was "on call" in emergencies. Amy was to start her job the upcoming Monday, and Jessie Miller started her job in two weeks' time. Claire Schonberger and Lucy Fuller had interviews to attend and both were hopeful.

"Don't look so distressed, Olive, I was just teasing with what I said to you before about being in love with your boss. It was silly of me."

Olive smiled at Jessie's flashing green eyes and said, "I know, I'm just a little concerned that one day he'll tell me that I don't have a job anymore and I won't see Leo again. I'm trying not to worry because I know that won't help anything. I keep telling myself if *Gott* wants me there then He will have me stay and if *Gott* wants me somewhere else, then He will put me somewhere else."

"You're right as usual. You were right for us to all advertise ourselves at the stall the other week. We're all going to get jobs out of it, it seems," Jessie said.

"*Jah—denke*, Olive," Amy agreed.

The other girls chimed in with thanking Olive, but were cut short when Dan placed a plate of chocolate fudge in the centre of their table. "You girls can be taste-testers and tell me what you think of our new chocolate delight."

Olive was sure the five of them were his favorite customers because he always showed them special attention. As always, he had a special smile for Lucy, which made her blush.

That night, Olive made sure she helped her *mudder* cook the dinner since she wasn't there to help on the weeknights. Their conversation quickly turned to Blake. "He's cranky with me all the time, *Mamm*. His *mudder*, Sonia, said it's because his wife died a year ago and he's upset with the world. It didn't help things that his *mudder* employed me without consulting him."

"*Jah*, that wouldn't help him. Men like to feel as though they're in charge."

"*Jah*, and they're not really, are they, *Mamm*?" Naomi had just walked into the room.

Mamm rolled her eyes. "Naomi, I'm trying to have a serious talk with your *schweschder*."

"I wasn't joking."

"Just sit down, be quiet and help Olive with the peas."

"Now, where were we?" *Mamm* asked Olive.

"You were saying men like to be in charge." Naomi giggled loudly.

"Up to your room!" *Mamm* ordered.

Naomi jumped to her feet and scowled. "I'm never included around here. Olive gets all the attention just because she's an ugly old maid."

Her mother picked up a wooden spoon and Naomi flew out of the room as fast as she'd ever moved before. "Go to your room," *Mamm* called after her. Once they heard the upstairs door closed, *Mamm* looked back at Olive. "She didn't mean it. You're not ugly. Nor are you an old maid."

"I don't care what she says. How will I help the situation with my boss being the way he is?"

"If someone is mean to you or rude and you remain polite, then that person will see that you aren't matching their ways."

"And?" Olive asked after her *mudder* left out the part about how that would help the situation.

With a laugh, her *mudder* added, "He will see how rude he's been and might correct his manners himself."

"That makes sense, I suppose; then I just pay his temper no mind?"

"*Jah*, that's right. Just be sure that working for an *Englischer* is not going to lead you into the ways of the world."

"*Jah*, I know. *Dat* has already mentioned that to me."

"We miss having you around the *haus*, but I suppose it had to happen some day. I hoped it would be for a different reason."

"*Mamm*, I know what you mean, but there are no men around for me. None of my friends have boys interested in them either. It seems in our community there are many more girls than men. That's why this job's a good idea. In the future, I might be able to buy myself a little *haus*, or at least afford a lease on one."

"Olive, I don't like hearing you speak of such things. Trust the *gut* Lord to bring you a *mann*."

Olive turned to her sweet *mudder* and smiled. "I will,

Mamm." She hoped she would marry someday, so her parents would be happy. But, Olive did not see how it could possibly happen for her. Not when she couldn't get Blake out of her mind.

Since it was raining heavily on Monday morning, Olive had one of her *bruders* drive her to Blake's house. She knew she'd have to think up indoor things she and Leo could do today. They normally played in the park or the yard, but now, with the approaching cold weather, she would have to think up new activities.

That morning, Blake seemed calmer, which was a surprising change. Had her prayers worked already? Leo had loved the pancakes she'd made and Blake had even stolen a couple before he left. She didn't say a word about it but had smiled secretly.

Even after talking it through with her friends on Saturday, Olive still could not get Blake's late wife out of her mind. As she wandered around the house, she realized that there were no pictures of his wife anywhere. She knew for a fact that *Englischers* often displayed photographs in their homes.

Without even thinking about it, her feet wandered from room to room. Every time she entered a new space, Olive searched for any sign of his wife, but there was none to be found. She knew there was nothing in either of Leo's rooms. She had never seen one picture or keepsake anywhere in the whole house. Olive decided that Blake must have loved her so much that he could not bear any reminder of her anywhere at all.

Leo would never remember his mother because of his young age, so it would be up to his family to tell him about her. Olive could not imagine not having her mother around when she had been growing up.

How would Leo ever learn what his mother was like? Would Blake speak of her or would his heartache prevent him from sharing memories with Leo? She knew it was none of her business, and they were *Englischers*, so most likely they did things in a very different manner.

Olive finished a few small chores around the house before Leo woke from his nap. He was so full of energy that Olive was irritated by the weather that kept them trapped indoors. She remembered an idea her *mudder* had used when she and her brothers couldn't go outside because of either the rain or the snow. Olive gathered a few sheets from the linen cupboard and went to work. Leo was excited about all the building she was doing and happily helped her. After they gathered some snacks from the kitchen, they climbed into their new tent.

Olive had moved the furniture to allow her to create the large tentlike structure. She pulled in some of Leo's toys and books. Together they enjoyed eating their snacks and playing with Leo's toys.

The sound of Leo's laughter was becoming her favorite sound. Olive didn't think she laughed as much with her girlfriends as she did with two-year-old Leo. From blocks, they moved on to reading a couple of stories. Leo loved the different voices she made for the characters and sat through two whole stories before his attention evaporated.

They heard the rain thundering down, but in their makeshift tent, Olive and Leo couldn't have cared less.

Olive looked at the clock. Blake would soon be home. "Come on, Leo, we have to clean up. Daddy will be home soon. You can help me with the dinner."

In a quiet moment, Blake had confessed he had grown up hardly seeing his own father because he had constantly worked. Maybe *Gott* had put her in this family to make a difference in their lives. She had offered to fix a meal for him and Leo on those evenings when he could make it home early enough.

During dinner that night, Blake said, "Tell me about being Amish, Olive."

It was a rare, quiet moment in which Leo was occupied trying to stab a pea with his fork.

"I don't know any other way of living." She looked up at Blake and realized that she had given him an insufficient answer. "What exactly would you like to know?"

"What are your thoughts on God? When I was younger, I went to church, searching for the meaning of life, but I never found it. I often wonder why we're all here."

"We're all here to live our lives for God. We won't be here for long; our real home is elsewhere with God."

"What is the purpose of us being here; why aren't we with God now if that's what He wants?"

"I guess He wants to find the faithful ones."

Blake looked down at his chicken and carefully cut a piece. "I was searching and then I couldn't find any answers. I guess I buried myself in my work."

"The difference with us is that we don't live for this life, but for the one we have with God."

"Hmm, I see that."

"We never know how long God will give us on this earth before He calls us home." As soon as she said it she wished she hadn't. Speaking of death would only remind him of Mona. She looked across at him, but he was busily eating as if he wasn't worried by what she said.

"Sometimes I feel my life's a treadmill. Like I'm a

mouse spinning on a wheel and going nowhere. I reach goals and they're not satisfying. Each one I reach no longer pleases me, and on and on I go. I know there's more. There's got to be more to this life than—" Their peace was shattered when Leo decided to see how far he could throw his vegetables. "No, Leo! You'll go to your room." Leo started to cry at the tone of Blake's voice. Then Blake shook his head and looked at Olive. "What would you do with him?" He nodded his head toward Leo.

"Take the peas from him." She looked at Leo, who'd stopped crying to watch the grownups. "I know you love to eat peas, but if you throw them you can't have them on your plate anymore."

He ignored Olive and rubbed his eyes.

"I think he's one tired little boy. We did a lot of activities today and he didn't have a nap."

"That must be it." He chuckled. "I like the way you make excuses for him."

Olive laughed. "I know it sounds like that, but it's true." Right on cue, Leo yawned.

After dinner, Olive cleared the dishes.

"I'll do that, Olive. You're off the clock. Leave them, and I'll take you home and do them when I come back."

"Are you sure?"

"Yes. And, the motion of the car might send somebody off to sleep."

Blake drove Olive home and there were no more questions about what it was like to be Amish. Olive was intrigued that he had seemed interested and had questioned the purpose of his life.

Chapter Nine

The next Friday when Olive got to Blake's house, he surprised her by announcing he was not going to work that day.

Olive's jaw dropped, and for a moment she was lost for words. "The whole day?" she eventually asked.

He nodded. It was a perfect seventy-degree morning with not a cloud in the sky.

"Do you want me to go home since you'll be here?" Olive offered looking down at Leo's excited face.

"No, I'd like you to come with us. We're going to find a nice spot for a swim in one of the creeks before the cold sets in."

"Might be a little late for that. The sun's out, but it's not that warm."

"It's only early in the day. It'll warm up. You're always telling me I should spend more time with him." Blake glanced at Olive briefly. "I guess his mother always did this stuff with him," he muttered. "I know you're right about me spending time with Leo since I hardly got to know my father. Perhaps you can pack us one of those picnics like you used to have as a child?"

Olive smiled. "I didn't think you were listening the other morning."

"The key to my success is to listen to the advice of others." He wagged a finger at her while a mischievous grin hinted around his lips. "Providing that the people who are giving the advice know what they are talking about."

"That's a compliment, is it? You think I know what I'm talking about when I speak about my childhood?"

"You're good with Leo; that has to come from your own upbringing since you've had no formal training."

Olive was quick to change the subject from her lack of training. "I'll pack us a *wunderbaar* picnic."

Blake chuckled.

"Before that, would you like coffee?" Olive asked.

"Absolutely." Blake sat on a kitchen stool. "Should we stop by your home, so you can get your swimsuit?"

Olive swung around to face him. "No, I don't wear anything like that. I mean, Amish don't ever wear them—ever."

"What do you swim in?"

She looked down at her clothes. "Just our clothes."

"Seems as though that would be dreadfully uncomfortable."

Olive shrugged and put the cup under the outlet of the built-in coffee machine. "We don't notice." She turned back toward him once the coffee cup was filled to the brim. "It's not considered modest to show too much skin."

"Ah," he said, as he nodded thanks for his coffee.

Feeling uneasy, Olive said, "I won't go into the water today. I only ever went for a swim on the hottest days."

"Daddy, come *wit'* us?" Leo asked his father in the broken words of a toddler.

Olive answered, "Yes, daddy's coming with us today, and we're going to have a picnic. Just like we had in the tent the other day." Olive could barely contain her smile at the thought of Blake spending time with his son. Maybe Blake's barriers were breaking down.

"Let me make a few phone calls while you load him into his car seat."

Leo squealed with excitement knowing that they were all going in the car.

After they got ready, Olive and Leo waited in the car for a long time while Blake made his phone calls. Leo tried to peel the car-seat straps off his shoulders. Just as Olive had given up on Blake and was opening the door to pull Leo out of the car, he climbed into the driver's seat.

"Everybody ready?" Blake turned the key in the ignition while Olive shut the car door.

"I've heard that the *Englisch* have play groups where their children can interact with other children," Olive said.

Blake glanced at Olive. "I suppose my mother mentioned that?"

Olive nodded.

"You can enroll him if you wish," Blake said.

"It's just that I notice that he keeps to himself even when we go to the park with other children. He doesn't speak to them."

Blake raised his eyebrows, which caused Olive to add, "I'm used to children playing well together and I notice that Leo likes to be by himself. Your mother mentioned something about it too."

"Sure, good idea."

Olive frowned at Blake. Was he listening to her at all?

After a few attempts to make a conversation, Olive had run out of things to say and Blake wasn't helping. It was now awkward. It wouldn't be as bad if he'd been unattractive. A handsome and wealthy, successful man like Blake would not even consider her as a suitable match even if she were *Englisch*. Men like him weren't likely to be attracted to a nanny, much less an Amish nanny who swam in clothing and closed her eyes to thank *Gott* before every meal. She wondered what the two of them would have in common or talk about if a marriage between them was ever allowed.

The more Olive thought about Blake, the faster her heart beat. Blake, in contrast, seemed comfortable and quiet in the driver's seat intently listening to a business radio show pouring through the speakers. His lack of small talk in the car made Olive unusually uncomfortable.

"Yay! We here!" Leo shouted with glee, once the car stopped.

Olive was relieved that the tension in the car had broken. Before Olive could open her door, Leo had nearly peeled himself from his five-point harness. Olive released the clips and pulled Leo from his car seat, while trying to balance the picnic basket and tote bag on her other arm. Blake must have noticed because he took Leo from her arms.

Blake and Leo chose a grassy spot on the bank to spread out the picnic blanket. The area they chose was not too close to the water, and had some pleasant shade from an old oak tree. Olive giggled when she saw Blake's fancy business shoes with traces of sand beading up on them. "You should change. I mean your shoes."

"I guess I should." Blake stood up, walked a little distance, took off his shoes and socks and rolled up his trousers slightly. When he came closer, he said, "I was going to go for a swim, but since it doesn't appear you will go in, then neither will I."

Olive smiled with relief. She did not know what she would do if she saw him half dressed.

"So, what kind of things did Leo's mom do with him?" she asked, trying to understand their situation better and learn something of Mona.

Blake looked away from her and shrugged. "The usual things."

"Leo needs to spend time with you. Maybe you can do something with him again tomorrow but by your-selves."

"I'm going to be busy tomorrow. Besides, I hire you to take care of Leo's needs."

Olive guessed that Blake would have his mother watch Leo tomorrow since it would be Saturday and she was only employed Monday through Friday. Maybe, he had to work tomorrow to make up for having today off.

The two of them sat in silence for a time and watched Leo run around. To get away from Blake, Olive took Leo into the water's edge to splash around. Her head hurt from trying to think of nice things to say to Blake, so she put him out of her mind and enjoyed playing with Leo.

"We should have gotten something to eat some-where," Blake muttered under his breath.

Olive laughed. "I've made all these sandwiches. It is a picnic and there wasn't much in the fridge today."

He scratched his head. "I've just started trying to stay away from gluten."

"Oh, I didn't know. How about we stop for ice cream on the way home?"

"Very well," Blake agreed.

It was no surprise to Olive that their trip to the ice-cream shop was much the same as their picnic had been. As they sat at a table in the ice-creamery, Blake occasionally corrected Leo about something and didn't say much else. Blake checked either his cell phone or his watch, as if he had somewhere more important to be.

The drive home was filled with even more painful silence. Leo fell asleep in the backseat, the result of hours of fresh air and a belly full of ice cream. The boring business podcast droned over the car's speakers, nearly lulling Olive to sleep.

Olive had a lot of time to think while she was in the car. She was tired from the day and grateful it was nearly over. If it weren't for sweet little Leo, she would surely turn down this job and Blake's money. What was the point of staying at the job with the crush she had on Blake when he didn't return that interest? But then again, if he did like her, that would be even more problematic.

Chapter Ten

It wasn't even dinnertime when they got home from their day out, but Leo was fast asleep. While Olive unpacked everything they had taken with them, Blake carried Leo to bed.

When Olive came inside to put the extra food into the refrigerator, she heard Blake's cell phone beep and he went into his den and came out ten minutes later.

Olive looked up to see a much happier Blake coming into the kitchen. "Good news?" she asked.

"Yes, that phone call was about a deal that I've just pulled off. I've been worried about it all day. A company was going to sign one of our contracts and balked at the last minute, but they've just signed it." Blake heaved a sigh.

She knew nothing of his business, nor did she desire to know about it, if it affected his moods so powerfully. "Leo didn't wake up when you put him down?"

Blake shook his head and smiled. "He's fast asleep."

Blake sat down in the kitchen instead of making phone calls in his den. "Are you happy here, Olive?"

"Yes, I love it here." She studied his face and no-

ticed he looked serious. Olive hoped that he would not
say he had no more need for her services. "Would you
like some coffee?"

He nodded. "Please. I was shocked when you first
came here and I saw that you were Amish. My mother
told me how good you were with Leo, but she said nothing about you being Amish." He cleared his throat then
added, "I wouldn't have thought you could take a job
such as this. I thought you Amish kept to yourselves."

"Many people work outside the community. We don't
socialize with *Englischers*, though."

Blake chuckled.

Olive spun around from scooping the coffee into
the stainless-steel compartment of the coffee maker.
"What's so funny?"

"I'm sorry, it just sounds funny to call people who
aren't Amish *Englischers*. I have heard it before though.
It's a funny word; I wonder where it came from."

Olive shrugged her shoulders; she knew, but was too
tired to tell him. Olive had noticed that the phone call
marked his change of demeanor.

"Tell me something about your family, Olive. You
know more about me than I know about you."

"I'm the second youngest. I have one younger sister
and five older brothers. Three are married and only two
of my brothers live at home."

"That's quite a crew."

"It's not big compared to some families in the community. We had a lot of fun together growing up, playing with all the animals. Mind you, it wasn't all fun; we
had a lot of chores to do as well." Olive giggled. "Well,
doing the chores was fun too, I guess. There was always something to laugh about. I'm closest with my

sister. She's three years younger and mostly annoying, but we're close for some reason."

"Did your parents have a working farm?"

Olive nodded. "Still do. My father has a dairy farm, and we children raised pigs and chickens. There were so many animals around when we were growing up."

"Since Leo has no brother or sisters and isn't likely to ever have any, I've been thinking of getting him a pet, maybe a dog. But, I'll wait until he's older."

Olive felt sad for Blake that he had so many years ahead of him and, from the sound of things, never wanted to get married again. He must have loved his wife so much that he could not contemplate the thought of loving another. "That would be a wonderful idea. He'd love to have a dog to take care of. It'll teach him responsibility and he'll have someone to care for. But I will look into that play group idea."

"Well, Olive, it sounds like you had the ideal child-hood; no wonder you're so good with Leo."

"Ah, you think I'm good with Leo?"

Blake threw back his head and laughed, but he did not answer her.

"You really do think I'm good with Leo?" Olive asked once more; she had to know.

"Of course, he adores you."

Olive smiled and knew that he was satisfied that he could trust her to look after his young son.

"Does that surprise you?" Blake asked.

Olive laughed a little. "You weren't too happy about me coming to work for you to begin with, were you?"

Blake smiled. "I was a little apprehensive since you had no experience."

"Your mother was insistent that I would be good

for the job. I told her that I had no experience and told her about my friend, Amy; she's the one who's got the experience with children. Your mother didn't want to know about anyone else."

"I suppose mother might know best after all." Blake chuckled. "I'm sorry I gave you such a hard time when you first arrived here. I guess I was being protective of Leo. It was all too sudden since my mother insisted she be the only one to look after Leo. I wasn't expecting her to go out shopping one day and hire a nanny."

"Mothers can be like that sometimes." Olive stared at the floor while she thought of her *mudder* who did things her own way. The coffee machine churned signaling that the coffee was ready. She pressed the button for his black coffee then placed the mug in front of him.

"Thanks." He nodded and took a sip. When he placed the mug back down on the table, he said, "You might as well finish early today, Olive. Leo won't wake up until much later."

"Are you sure? I could fix you some dinner." It was a couple of hours before the time he usually came home.

"No, you deserve a little time off. I'd drive you home if Leo weren't asleep."

"I don't mind riding the bike; it's kind of peaceful."

Olive pulled her coat up around her neck and set off toward home. By the time she was a little way up the road, her mind kept drifting toward Blake. Sometimes she'd caught him looking at her differently, and had done so for days. *Is he starting to like me?* She hoped so.

Chapter Eleven

The next Monday, Olive arrived at Blake's house to find Sonia there. In the early days, Sonia had called in nearly every day to check on her, but now her visits were less frequent—most likely thanks to all those video cameras Blake had installed around the house. He still hadn't admitted to Olive that they were there. Leo rushed toward Olive when Sonia met her at the door; a few minutes later, he settled down and played with some blocks in the living room.

When Olive noticed that Blake was not frantically rushing about, she asked Sonia, "Has Blake left already?"

"Yes, he left about five minutes ago. It's so much quieter without him, isn't it?"

Olive knew at that moment she was in trouble. She had a burning crush on her boss. Otherwise, she wouldn't have been so disappointed she wouldn't see him until the evening. "Yes, it is a lot quieter. Can I get you tea or coffee, Sonia?"

"Tea, please."

"Mom, mom," Leo muttered while he was playing.

"Leo, you must never say that." Leo looked up at Sonia with a look of confusion.

Olive was about to head to the kitchen when she saw and heard their exchange. *Be quiet, Olive. It's none of your business,* she told herself. She was sure Leo was just mumbling things. He didn't know anyone as Mom and couldn't have known what the word meant, so what was so terrible?

As she made the tea, Olive knew she had to find out more about Leo's mother. Should she dare to ask Sonia when Sonia'd had such a reaction to Leo mentioning her? Why wouldn't Blake and his mother encourage Leo to talk about Mona? Something felt wrong.

When Leo's grandmother joined her in the kitchen, leaving Leo playing in the living room, Olive saw that as an opportunity to ask some questions.

It was Sonia who spoke first. "Olive, I saw the look on your face just now when I scolded Leo for what he was saying." Olive opened her mouth slightly, and then Sonia flung up her hand. "Don't even try to deny it; I can read you like a book." Sonia sat down at the kitchen table. "You see it would upset Blake to hear Leo mention the word."

"But don't you think that's a little unrealistic? Leo should be able to speak about his mother and should learn of the great love that his parents once shared. The love that brought him into the world."

"Humph. Great love? Well, yes. I mean…" Sonia stammered, her kind eyes closing for a second. Sonia opened her eyes and said, "Heavens. I guess it won't hurt to tell you. There's not much to the story really. We don't share the details because we don't want Leo to be hurt when he's older and finds out the truth about his mother." Sonia leaned forward and spoke in a low voice so Leo wouldn't be able to hear. "I suppose it's time you found out. Blake's wife was killed when she was running off with Blake's good friend. They were driving off together, had an accident and she was killed instantly."

Olive gasped and held her stomach.

"The first Blake knew of things was two minutes after he arrived home one night and police officers knocked on the door and gave him the news. He's never been the same. She ran off with no word. All her things were gone, money had been cleaned out of their joint account and everything. Her lover had been driving, and he was badly injured. I'm not sure what happened to him afterward. Blake has never mentioned his name and I'm not about to ask."

"Where was Leo at the time?"

"Mona brought him over to my house saying she had a doctor's appointment and would pick him up later that day." Sonia looked into the distance. "I remember thinking at the time that she seemed overdressed to be going to the doctor."

"Thank you for telling me, Sonia. It all makes sense now. I mean Blake's anger."

Sonia nodded. "He's a broken man."

"I wondered why there was no sign of her anywhere in the house." Olive wondered what they would tell Leo about his mother when he got older. Would he ever learn what his mother was like. She must have had good qualities; would he ever learn of those? *It is none of my business,* Olive reminded herself.

"Left behind was a little note and her little boy. What kind of woman would choose another man over her own son?" She sighed. "I guess we should've seen it coming. Leo's mother was always so very needy of Blake's attention, like she was still a child. When he couldn't give her one hundred and ten percent of his time, she went looking elsewhere."

"My mother always says that there are two sides to everything."

Sonia scoffed. "What that woman did was unforgivable. Nothing in the world could justify what she did, running away like that and leaving Leo."

"I can imagine how this has been hard on Blake, but even harder on Leo. A little boy needs his mother," Olive agreed as she poured the tea into Sonia's cup.

"I don't blame him for taking down those pictures. What man wouldn't? They were just painful reminders of Mona's infidelity."

Olive finally understood what Blake and Leo had been through.

"There were photos up somewhere?" She'd been right about that.

"Yes, there were photos in the living room. I'll show you a picture of the three of them. They made such a beautiful family. I've got one in my handbag." Sonia trotted over to the other side of the kitchen to get her bag and retrieved a small photo from inside.

Olive took the picture and studied it. The woman was fair and small, not unlike herself, yet this woman was most attractive. Blake looked years younger even though the photo was taken just over a year ago. "Leo had his curls even at that age." Olive smiled.

Sonia snatched it back. "Mona looks a little like you."

"I suppose; we've both got light brown hair and fair skin."

"And you've got the same slight build. Hmm." Sonia tossed the photo onto the kitchen counter beside her handbag. Sonia didn't stay long after her cup of tea.

In the late afternoon, Olive noticed that the small photo was still where Sonia had tossed it. Leo was drawing at his small table in the living room. She picked up the photo to hide it so Blake wouldn't see it. As she picked it up, she studied Leo's mother's face.

"What have you got there?"

Olive clutched the photo and spun around. "Blake, you startled me. I didn't hear you come in."

"I came in the front way. What has you so interested?" Frowning, she placed the photo down on the counter.

How would she explain this?

Blake's eyes fell to the image of his late wife and his face flushed red. He bellowed, "What in tarnation are you doing with that?"

She could feel tears well in her eyes; no one had ever yelled at her like that. Her breathing grew heavy as she tried to talk herself out of crying. She could not speak.

"Well? Answer me."

Tears flowed down Olive's cheeks. She'd been holding it in for weeks; he'd been so horrible to her at times and she'd done her best, but this was too much. She covered her face with both her hands as tears streamed from her eyes.

"I'm so sorry." Blake stepped close and wrapped his warm arms around her.

She leaned into the hardness of his chest and cried some more. When her tears subsided, she stepped away from him. He reached for the box of tissues behind him and handed her some.

"Your mother told me about your wife and showed me the photo. She left it here by mistake. I was only looking at it." Olive dabbed her eyes. "I was going to hide it somewhere so you wouldn't see it and be sad."

Blake put his head down. "I'm a beast. Forgive me, Olive. I've upset you."

"Yes, you've upset me and you upset me most days." Olive sniffed some more and wiped her eyes.

"I've been intolerable. There's no excuse for my behavior. I should have told you about Leo's mother. It wasn't a secret; I suppose it's the reason for my temper."

Leo ran into the room and looked at both of them. He hugged Olive around her knees, which made her feel better.

"I'll drive you home, Olive. We can put your bike in the trunk."

Olive nodded and sniffed some more. "I'll splash some cold water on my face, so my family doesn't see me like this."

When they arrived at her parents' house, she glanced over at Blake to thank him for driving her. She noticed he was staring at her with a soft look in his eyes.

"Olive, would you come to dinner with me one night? Just you and me?"

Olive felt as though she could not breathe for an instant. She was attracted to him, but would he always be angry? Was she willing to compromise herself to go on a date with an *Englisch* man? "You mean like a date?"

"Exactly like a date—because it will be a date," he answered, now looking at her lips.

"I don't know."

He looked away. "I see."

"Blake, it isn't as simple as that. I can't go to dinner with you. You're not Amish."

He nodded, still not looking at her. "I see," he repeated, his voice almost a whisper.

Olive opened the door. "I'd better go. Someone's sure to be watching us from the window."

Blake opened his door. "I'll get your bike out for you."

Olive turned to say goodbye to Leo, but he was already asleep in the backseat. She met Blake at the back of the car.

"I always seem to be apologizing to you."

She shook her head. "There's no need." She reached out for the handlebars of the bike and in the dark, she put her hand on his. She left it there and did not pull away.

He lightly touched her hand with his other one, and whispered, "Don't give up on me, Olive." He slid his hands away, and she clutched the bike to steady it as he walked back to the car. She wheeled her bike toward the barn while she listened to the hum of his car as he drove away.

"Was that Blake?" her older brother Elijah asked when she walked into the house.

Olive nodded. "He said it was too cold for me to ride my bike."

"Where? Where is he?" Naomi came flying down the stairs and looked out the window. "I missed him," she said as she stared out the window at the car that was now at the end of the driveway.

"I'll drive you and fetch you from now on," Elijah said firmly.

"Denke." Olive knew that her brother was not con-

cerned with the cold, he was concerned with her getting too close to her *Englisch* employer.

"You're early today," Olive's *mudder* said as she walked into the kitchen to help with the dinner.

"*Jah*, I am. Blake drove me home because it was too cold."

"You've ridden home on colder nights." Her *mudder* peered into her face. "Have you been crying?"

Naomi skipped into the room. "She's been driven home by her new boyfriend."

"Naomi. Don't say that," *Mamm* scolded. "Set the table, Naomi." *Mamm* turned her attention back to Olive. "Have you been crying?" she asked again.

"Just a cold coming on, I think. That's why he drove me home." Normally Olive told her *mudder* everything, but tonight she did not have the energy to explain the whole situation. Could Blake be in love with her? She had controlled her attraction toward him, but if he felt the same that would make things difficult.

"I wish I'd seen him," Naomi grumbled as she placed the knives and forks on the table.

"He's just my boss, Naomi."

"Yeah, right."

Throughout the dinner, Olive could not keep her mind off Blake and the warmth of his hand on hers. They'd shared a moment. How much longer could she contain her feelings and her attraction toward him? When she was alone in her room, she wondered how different her world would be if Blake was Amish.

She shook her head to rid herself of silly notions. Blake was not Amish and there was only one chance in a million he would ever change his life and become

Amish. *People do though,* she told herself. *I've seen five families become Amish in my lifetime. Jah, whole families, but not a single man with a child,* she argued with herself. She recalled Sonia telling her there'd been many women who'd fallen in love with Blake. She wasn't special; she was just one of many.

Chapter Twelve

When Olive woke the next morning, Blake was still on her mind. How could she go back there when she'd cried in his arms? Still in bed, she shut her eyes tightly and remembered the feel of being held in his strong arms, her head leaning into the hardness of his chest.

What had he meant when he said not to give up on him? Most likely he meant not to leave the job over his temper outbursts. *Jah, that's all it would be,* she thought, wishing he had meant something regarding a deeper relationship, perhaps a future romance.

Blake was right there to open the door for her when she knocked on it. She looked down to see Leo crouched behind Blake, his chubby hands clasped around his father's ankles.

"Good morning, Leo."

"Good morning, Ollie."

Olive giggled as she usually did when Leo said her name. She was nervous to see Blake again, but his ready smile put her at ease.

"Since I've got an early start I'd better make a move. If I can, I'll be home early."

"That would be good, wouldn't it, Leo?" Olive bent down to Leo's height.

"Ya." He swung onto her neck freeing his father.

"I want to speak to you, too, when I get home," Blake said to Olive.

Olive smiled and nodded, then Leo and she watched Blake as he walked to his car.

Throughout the day, Olive wished that Blake had not mentioned he wanted to speak to her about something; she could not stop worrying over what it might be. Did he want to end her employment? All she could do was wait until he returned. That day the cleaning lady arrived at the same time as the food delivery. Once Olive put all the food away, she took Leo outside to play, so they would not get in the housekeeper's way.

When Blake returned home, he played with Leo for a while and then sat down on the couch with Olive. "I want to explain about Mona."

Olive blinked rapidly and looked away. "It's not necessary to say anything."

"Yes, it is. I was not a good husband to her. I left her alone with Leo and she got lonely. I was busy at work and even when I was here, I was either on the laptop or the cell phone. It's my fault, what she did; I hardly spoke to her. She would have been incredibly lonely. She was sweet and not some horrible demanding woman like my mother probably told you. Everyone has their limitations, and Mona and I had reached ours."

Olive nodded.

Blake continued, "I've got deep regret over what I did. I wasn't a proper husband. All I wanted was a family. I took what I had for granted. I kept thinking we could have it all if only I worked a little harder or a little longer. My idea was that if I worked hard now, in a few years, we could enjoy ourselves without me having to work so hard." He shrugged his shoulders. "Now, she's gone. I have Leo and he has no mother."

"Now is all we have," Olive said.

"I've realized that. Learned it the hard way."

Olive squirmed in her seat. "I should get going; it's getting late."

"I'll drive you."

"*Nee,* my *bruder* is waiting for my call and then he'll come get me." Olive realized that in her nervousness she had just spoken a few words of Pennsylvania Dutch to an *Englischer.* "I'm sorry. You probably didn't understand a word of that."

"I did."

She smiled and then headed to the phone and picked up the receiver. She hoped that Elijah would be in the barn when her call came through, so she wouldn't have to wait at Blake's house any longer than necessary. He answered on the third ring. When Elijah told her that he already had the horse and buggy ready to leave, Olive heaved a sigh of relief and ended the call.

"I've disappointed you, haven't I?" Blake said.

"It's not for me to judge. Your personal life is none of my concern. I'm just Leo's nanny; I'm concerned for him, that's all."

"I had hoped that you would like to be a little more than that."

Olive shook her head. "Nothing could ever work between us. We're too different. The Amish have different levels of commitment to marriage than it appears other people do. I would never get married unless it was for life; it can be no other way."

"It seems that I'm always hurting the people I care for."

Olive was uneasy hearing him speak of his late wife and their unhappiness. "I'll wait outside for my brother."

"Olive, don't leave like this. I'm sorry if I've said too much."

"No, you haven't. I'm pleased you told me. It's best I wait outside. My brother won't be far away."

Olive said goodbye to Leo and hurried down the driveway. The weather was colder, but Olive was too amazed by what she had just learned to take any notice. Her *familye* were right to be concerned about her working amongst the *Englisch*. She hoped that she hadn't put any of her friends in a similar situation with her silly idea that they should all become maids. Two of them had already gotten jobs with *Englischers*.

Olive wanted to share what she had learned about Blake, so she could have the benefit of someone else's opinion, but in whom could she confide? Her *mudder* would never let her go back there if she breathed a word of it and *Mamm* learned of her feelings for Blake. She could tell one of her friends and the one who would tell her what she really thought would be Jessie. She would see Jessie at the gathering on Sunday. No, it was too long to wait. Olive decided to visit Jessie before then, but she would have to wait until her day off on Saturday.

Chapter Thirteen

All was quiet when Olive arrived at Jessie's *haus* on Saturday morning. She walked around to the back of the house and stuck her head through the door. "Jessie?"

"Is that you, Olive?"

Olive stepped through the door. "*Jah*, it's me. Where are you?"

"I'm upstairs in my bedroom. Come up."

It appeared Jessie's parents were out. Jessie's mother was always in the kitchen, it seemed, and usually on a Saturday Jessie's father was reading on the couch in the living room. Olive made her way through the kitchen, then the living room, and then walked up the wooden stairs. She found Jessie in her room, dressed except for her prayer *kapp*.

"I'm running a little late today." Jessie ran a brush through her wavy hair.

"Are you going somewhere?"

"*Nee*, I've nothing to do but some chores today."

"Oh, Jessie," Olive said as she flopped down on Jessie's bed.

Jessie rushed to sit beside her. "What is it? Job not going well?"

"I don't know where to begin. It's almost too awful to speak of."

"Tell me."

Olive looked into Jessie's intelligent green eyes and knew she could tell her the whole sorry thing.

After she told Jessie everything about her feelings for Blake, being held in his arms, being asked out on a date, his confession of how he treated his wife, Jessie stared into the distance as she took it all in.

"Say something, Jessie. I thought you'd give me some advice or tell me to leave the job or something."

"It's not the first time one of us has fallen in love with an *Englischer*."

Olive nodded. "Should I stay there?"

"You can't just change jobs because of something like that." Jessie looked deeply into Olive's eyes. "Unless, he feels the same way. Does he?" Jessie raised her eyebrows.

Olive winced. "That's the trouble. He's as good as admitted he likes me. Otherwise, he wouldn't have asked me on a date. He even said it would be a date. Of course, I refused, but I wanted to go."

"*Ach*. That complicates things. Maybe you should leave. The bishop says we should not make a place for sin. *The closer we go to the edge of the cliff the more likely we are to fall off.* That's what the bishop said just last Sunday."

Olive nibbled on a fingernail. "*Jah*, I remember." This was not what Olive wanted to hear. Why wasn't Jessie telling her it would be okay to stay? "Maybe if I pray about it things will turn out well."

Jessie screwed up her face. "You mean you want to marry him or something?"

"Don't be like that, Jessie. Some *Englischers* have joined the community."

"*Jah*, but more often it's the Amish who leaves the community." When Olive did not respond, Jessie added, "Has he ever said anything about becoming Amish?"

"He's asked some questions about *Gott*."

"Well, what does he do for work? Could he still work if he joined us—if the bishop allowed him to join?"

Olive took a deep breath. "I'm not sure what he does. I think he does something at an office somewhere."

Jessie put her head in her hands. "Olive, you're not thinking straight. Just because there's no men in the community for us doesn't mean you go out looking amongst the *Englischers*."

"*Nee*, Jessie. I wasn't doing that at all." Olive grabbed Jessie's hand. "Jessie, I had a thought on the way over here."

"What was that?" Jessie smiled.

"What about my *bruder* for you? He asked where I was going this morning and I noticed a funny look on his face when I said I was coming here to see you."

Jessie gave a little giggle. "Really? He never looks twice at me."

"Let me see what I can do." Olive thought that one of them amongst their group of friends should be married and her *bruder* Elijah was a fine man.

"*Nee*, Olive, don't you say one thing to him. I'd be embarrassed."

"Better to be embarrassed once and then be married." Olive giggled. "You've got nothing to lose. I'll ask him what he thinks of you. Maybe he could take you on a buggy ride."

"Wasn't he courting Becca Miller?"

"A long time ago, but that didn't work out. Think about it; we could be sisters."

When Olive was leaving Jessie's *haus*, she felt no better.

Maybe because she wanted Jessie to say that she thought it was alright for her to stay working for Blake.

"I start my new job tomorrow at the bed-and-breakfast. Say a prayer for me? The boss is scary."

Olive giggled. "You'll do fine."

"I hope so."

When Monday morning came, Olive felt as if it had been two months rather than two days since she had seen both Leo and Blake. When she got to the door, it swung open and Blake filled the doorway. "Hello, Blake."

"I'm glad you came back. I was a little worried you might not."

Olive said nothing as she walked inside. She looked around for Leo. "It's very quiet in here."

"My mother's got Leo." Olive frowned.

"I need to talk to you, Olive. Let's sit in the living room."

This is where I get fired. I'll have to look for another job, she thought as she sank into the couch.

Blake sat heavily next to her. "I've told my mother everything. I told her that I was responsible for what Mona did due to my being neglectful."

Olive opened her mouth to speak, but Blake contin-

ued, "I've righted my wrongs. I will tell Leo the truth
of the matter when he is old enough."

"Why are you telling me all this? I'm just the nanny."

"There's a saying, and I don't know if you've heard it.
'You don't know what you've got until it's gone.' I had
a family. I had everything and I didn't value it. Now it's
the only thing that I want." Blake moved a little closer to
Olive. "I want to be a better man for you, Olive. You're
a genuine person and I want that in Leo's life, to have
that in my life. I want to be the best man I can be for
Leo, and with you beside me I know it will happen."

"Me beside you?" Olive frowned.

"Come on that date with me, Olive?"

Olive wanted to scream yes. She wanted to more
than anything and if he were Amish, she would have
said yes. "You know I can't, Blake."

"And why is that?"

"You aren't Amish."

"And if I were?"

Olive smiled at him and then looked down at her
hands in her lap. "Then I'd happily go on a date with
you."

"You truly would?" He seemed happy and a little
surprised she'd said so.

"Yes."

"Then, how do I go about becoming Amish?"

Olive looked up into his eyes and no words came.
Had she heard correctly? She found her voice and asked,
"Did you say, how do you become Amish?"

He nodded. "Yes, I did. How do I go about that?"

Olive giggled. "You'd change your whole way of life
for me to go on a date with you?"

"Not just a date. I would hope for more, of course. I

would want us to marry someday if you'd have a cranky old man like me, but I would change and lose this crankiness. I'd be the man I used to be. I'd give management of my business over and relax for a bit."

Olive studied his face to see if he was joking. He surely couldn't be serious.

"I'm determined to be the best man I can be. Since I left God a long time ago, my life hasn't been right. He's calling me back to Him. He confirmed it when I saw you standing there the very first day you came to work for me."

"Ah, was that why you had such a temper toward me?"

Blake smiled. "I was running away from God's call on my life. I guess I might have been resisting Him and taking it out on you."

"You don't have to be Amish for your life to be right with God. I probably shouldn't say this, but I'm sure there are different paths to the one God. You don't have to join the community."

Blake flicked his eyes up to the ceiling and said, "I know what you're saying, but I feel it's right for me and the only way I can get rid of the ties that bind me to earthly things. I need a complete cut off, a complete break. Everything clicked for me when you told me about your childhood. I want Leo to have the best life possible. I miss having a family, a proper family. There's something I haven't told you yet; I paid a visit to your bishop on Saturday afternoon."

"You did?"

Blake nodded. "We had a long talk. I have respect for your bishop; he's an insightful man."

Olive stared into his face and wondered if he was joking. "What did he say?"

"I found out what I have to do to join the Amish."

Olive blew out a deep breath. *Is this really happening? Or, is he a man who is prone to whims?*

"I won't disappoint you. I'm a changed man and I'll keep changing, improving until I'm the best I can be."

This was everything for which she had hoped.

He cleared his throat. "You know, the bishop said that it would be at least six months before we could court. I wouldn't have to give up my business, but he suggested trading it for something that would cause me fewer headaches. I could sell my business interests and do something else. Anyway, business aside, would that be long enough for you to learn to like me enough to court you—six months?" Blake asked.

Olive wanted to tell him exactly how she felt, but instead, she asked, "What does your mother say about it?"

"My mother approves of anything involving you. That's why she's agreed to watch Leo for the day. I'm determined to prove myself to you."

Olive stared at him open-mouthed.

"Olive, I'm a practical man. All I'm asking of you is one date before I join the Amish. Leo and I will have to live with a family for three months. It will be another three months before I'm permitted to court you, so that's six months at least before I can prove myself worthy. Will you have lunch with me today before I embark on that journey?"

"So, you have decided to join us? You really want that? I mean, have you truly thought through every aspect?"

"Yes. Come to lunch with me and we'll talk about it?" Blake asked once again.

Olive looked into his pleading dark eyes and smiled. "All right, I guess one lunch couldn't hurt. But, only if we're clear that it is not a date; it's just a lunch."

He put a strong arm around her and hugged her close.

She looked up at him, and asked, "Does this mean I'll be losing my job?"

He wrapped his other arm around her and held her tight. "You'll be getting much, much more. That is, if you'll want me in six months' time. I'll do everything in my power to ensure you do. I'm not the impossibly awful man you first met. I'm not like that deep down inside." He shrugged a little. "I've had too many worries. I'll show you the real me and if you'll accept me, I'll look after you and give you a good and happy life."

Olive looked into his dark eyes and sent a silent prayer of thanks to *Gott* for answering her prayers better than she could have hoped.

When she did not answer him, Blake said, "You'll have time to get used to the idea of marrying me, and I'll have time to be the person I was meant to be."

"Marrying? Do we even know each other well enough?"

"I know what I want. I've always known what I want, and I want you. My sincere hope is that in time, you'll feel that way about me too."

Olive knew he was just like his mother and would not take no for an answer. In her heart, she felt she knew the real Blake. Glimpses of him had shone through. Smiling, Olive said, "If you're serious about me, I'll wait those six months."

A smile lit his serious face. "I am. And, when I move

in with the Hiltys like your bishop has arranged, you'll see that I'm serious. First, I'll have to break the news to my mother. One chance is all I'm asking from you. One chance and to wait for me until I fulfil all I need to do to be baptized into your community."

"I'll wait, of course I will." He nodded, still smiling.

Everything always turns out just the way in which it was meant. Olive couldn't wait to tell everyone. The first person she'd tell would be Jessie.

The next Saturday, Olive arranged to collect Jessie and take her into town to meet the girls. Olive had allowed her younger sister, Naomi, to go with her as long as she was quiet and didn't dominate the conversation at the cafe.

When Jessie got into the buggy, Olive blurted out her news. She'd wanted to wait until all the girls were together, but she couldn't help telling Jessie.

"Are you serious?"

"*Jah*, I am."

"*Nee.*"

"It's true. I can hardly believe it either."

Jessie was silent for a couple of moments and Olive hoped she wouldn't disapprove.

"This is the best news ever. And, he proposed?"

"Well, I guess it was a proposal. He said he wants us to marry but he knows there are things he has to do first."

"Olive, things like this just don't happen. Well, I suppose that's wrong, they do."

"I'm glad you're pleased."

"I am. Did you tell him about *Gott*?"

"*Nee*, he started talking first. He's been searching for Him."

Jessie leaned over and hugged Olive, causing Olive to giggle. "I'm so happy for you. Wait 'til the other girls find out. They'll be so surprised."

"I know."

Once the girls were all sitting down at the coffee shop, Olive contained her news while they all shared what was going on in their lives.

"I don't know how long I'll have my job for," said Claire.

"Why not?" Amy asked.

"It's the daughter-in-law. She keeps staring at me and correcting everything I do. She wants to get rid of me I just know it."

"Don't worry," Lucy said. "You'll get something else if you have to leave."

Claire looked down into her coffee and stirred it. "*Jah,* I know I will. I just like the old couple, you know?"

"I like the people I'm working for too," Amy said. "Only thing is, I'm certain... I'm not certain, but I think *Dat* doesn't like me working for *Englischers* and he could tell me to leave at any time."

Olive listened to the girls talking and felt bad having good news. Then Jessie said, "I'm starting a new job soon at a bed-and-breakfast."

"That's so good, Jessie," Amy said.

Jessie then hushed all the girls as two of them started to talk at once. "Olive has good news."

They all looked at Olive and she giggled. "I don't know how to say this or where to start."

"Just say it or I'll say it for you," Jessie said.

"You know what news she's got, Jessie?" Amy asked.

"She does," Olive said. "I couldn't keep it in. Blake is joining our community and he wants to marry me."

A hush of silence swept over the girls. Their faces were expressionless, except for Jessie who'd been smiling since Olive told her the news.

"What do you think?" Olive asked.

Amy's face was the first to break into a smile. "We're stunned. Really?"

"*Jah*, really," Jessie said, on Olive's behalf.

Naomi couldn't help herself. "*Jah*, our folks said they're pleased, but they're being cautious until he actually joins us officially."

Olive gave her a look that said "keep quiet," and then said to the girls, "By the time he told me, he'd been to the bishop and everything."

Amy jumped up, walked over and hugged her. "This is *wunderbaar* news. I'm so shocked, that's all."

Olive giggled. "I was surprised too. I expected to hear I was fired, but it's really happening."

Then all the girls hugged Olive and congratulated her.

"It'll be some time before we can get married, that is, if he stays. He could find it all too difficult."

"From what you said, he's a businessman with a brain in his head. He would've made a calculated decision," Amy said.

Olive nodded. "That's true, but living it can be difficult. You don't know what something's like until you've lived it."

"We'll all believe for you, Olive. This is so wonder-

fully romantic. Don't let doubts creep into your heart."
Claire covered Olive's hand with hers.

The girls all agreed and Olive looked around at their
faces and silently thanked God she was blessed with
such friends. And soon, God willing, Blake would be
her husband and she'd have a readymade family with
her stepson, Leo.

Chapter Fourteen

Jessie Miller's heart pounded as she rushed to the B&B to get to her new job on time. She knew Mrs. Billings was a stickler for everything including punctuality; she'd told Jessie as much in the job interview.

Her boss had seen Jessie's job flyer at the farmers' market some time ago and asked her to come for an interview. Mrs. Billings said she was prepared to give her four days a week, and if she did a good job it would become five days.

Mrs. Billings had once employed an Amish girl, so she knew they were hard workers and was happy to employ another. Since Jessie had never worked as a maid before, Mrs. Billings said she'd arrange for her to "shadow" one of the other maids for the first week.

Jessie stepped through the open double doors and looked directly into the pale brown eyes of Mrs. Billings. She was a tall slim lady with platinum blonde hair swept up on her head; everything about her was neat and perfect.

"Miss Miller, right on time. Come, I'll show you where the cleaning room is—where you'll be working from." Without waiting for a reply, Mrs. Billings strode down the wide hallway talking as she went. Jessie exchanged smiles with the receptionist and followed Mrs. Billings. "You're working with my best maid, Linda, today. If you do exactly what she tells you, you'll get along just fine." At the end of the hallway, Mrs. Billings stopped and looked down. "These steps lead to the cleaning room. You might have to dip your head." Mrs. Billings walked down the steps, opened the rough wooden door and then walked through.

Jessie followed and looked around the room to see two big machines, brooms of all sizes, mops, buckets and a variety of solutions.

"This is where we keep all the equipment you'll be needing. If you wait here, I'll send Linda to you."

"Very good, thank you. I'll work hard for you, Mrs. Billings."

Mrs. Billings spun around and looked her up and down without a hint of a smile. "I expect nothing less." With that, she spun back and walked out the door.

Jessie rubbed her forehead. Mrs. Billings had seemed much nicer during the job interview.

"Hello, Jessie."

Jessie looked toward the door at a heavyset woman with a pleasantly plump face and a ready smile. Jessie guessed her to be around thirty-five years of age. "You must be Linda."

"That's right. I'll show you the ropes. First thing every mornin' we fill up the carts." Linda grabbed the handle of one of the two carts at the side of the room. "We push 'em from room to room. That way, we don't go runnin' back to the cleaning room all day long. We have everything we need in the cart."

"Got it." Jessie nodded.

"Have a look at how this cart is set up. This is what you'll need."

As she had a good look at everything in the cart, trying to commit it to memory, Jessie noticed Linda staring at her.

"Done anything like this before, have ya?"

"I've done plenty of housework at home; I've never cleaned for someone else. This is my first job."

"Old Mrs. Billings is okay to work for as long as you don't go getting on the wrong side of her. She likes everything just so. The beds all have to be made exactly the same way, with the folded over corners and no wrinkles. Anyway, I'll show you how to make a proper bed."

"Oh, I know how to do that." Jessie frowned.

Linda scoffed. "Not the way Mrs. Billings likes 'em you don't. Now, you'll get along fine in this place if you do everythin' the way she tells you. Some people haven't lasted a day."

Jessie felt her shoulders tighten with tension. She was usually confident, but the thought of working away from the community and for people she didn't know had sapped the confidence out of her. "I'll do what you say."

Smiling, Linda finished filling up the second cart. "Now, we have to lift the cart up those stairs, and it's a job for two. We won't need the second one today. She's not making you wear a uniform then?" Linda asked in the midst of their struggle with the cart.

Glancing at Linda's black and white striped dress and then down at her own Amish clothing, she shook her head. "Mrs. Billings never said I'd have to wear a uniform. I couldn't wear something other than what I'm wearing anyway."

"Amish?"

"Yes." Jessie found it hard to speak while she pushed the cart up the stairs.

Linda pulled the cart from the top of the stairs. "I suspect she might have known you couldn't wear anything else. We had an Amish girl working here some time ago."

"Yes, Mrs. Billings told me that."

"Let me give you a hand, Linda," a male voice said from behind them.

Jessie looked up to see who belonged to the deep, rich voice. He was in his late twenties, with soft brown eyes.

Linda stepped back. "Mighty kind of ya, Donovan." He heaved the cart up in one go.

"You should do this every morning for us. Better still, tell yer mother it's not practical to keep the carts down there. It's too hard to bring 'em up and down each day. I've been tellin' 'er that for years and she hasn't listened to me. You should talk to her."

With his eyes fixed on Jessie, he said, "You know what she's like. There's no space unless she loses one of the bedrooms, and she's not about to do that since it means she'll be losing money." He glanced over at Linda and then back to Jessie.

"Donovan, this is Jessie. It's 'er first day—maybe 'er last when she sees how hard your mother works us."

"I don't mind hard work; really I don't. I'm quite used to it." Jessie walked up the stairs to join them.

"You are?" Donovan stared at Jessie with a lopsided smile on his face.

She tried to work out why he was staring at her with such amusement.

Linda gave Jessie no time to respond. "She's Jessie,

like I said, and we've got work to do. We can't stand around and natter all the day long. C'mon, Jessie." Linda walked away quickly with one hand wheeling the cart behind her. Jessie had no choice but to follow Linda even though she would have much rather stayed and talked to Donovan.

Linda knocked on the first door at the other end of the hallway and when no one answered she unlocked the door and walked in. "Come in, Jessie. Now, we leave the cart outside, and the first thing we do is empty the trash and strip the beds."

"Was that Mrs. Billings' son?"

"Yeah, Donovan. He owns the restaurant." Linda stopped what she was doing and took one step closer to Jessie. "He's a player. You'll do good to keep away from that one. He's friendly and all that, but he's not the kind of man who'd be right for the likes of you."

Jessie frowned. "Oh, no. I wasn't thinking of anything like that. Just curious, that's all."

Linda gave her a long hard look. "Just warnin' ya."

The morning was taken up with learning how to make beds the "Mrs. Billings way" and finding out what cleaning products to use for each particular task. Jessie had to remember exactly how Mrs. Billings preferred everything arranged in the rooms. The bath towels had to each be folded into a fan shape, and they were to be arranged just so on the beds with three rose-shaped pink soaps on the top of each. The end of each toilet paper roll was to be folded into a triangle; the washcloths and hand towels had their own hanging bars and had to be perfectly square with a washcloth precisely centered over each hand towel.

"One whole hour for lunch is what you get. Or you can take half an hour and leave half an hour earlier in the afternoon. We're fifteen minutes' walk to town, or you can stay 'ere and eat on the grounds."

"I brought my lunch with me."

"I'm driving into town if you wanna come with."

"Thank you, but I'd rather stay here."

Linda shrugged. "Please yaself."

At lunchtime, Jessie took her sandwiches out into the garden. In the distance, she saw a white wooden bench under a spreading willow tree. "That's where I'll eat today," she said aloud.

She sat down on the seat, pleased with the silence as she unwrapped her chicken sandwiches. It was far more difficult cleaning for someone else than it was for her *mudder*. Her *mudder* was only concerned that everything was clean. There were no little decorations and fancy things at home like there were at the B&B. Neither were there set routines on how things should be performed and particular places in which things should be placed.

She looked up to see Donovan striding toward her. "Hello, Jessie, how was your first day?"

"Hello. It isn't over yet. So far, it seems to be fine."

"Going from that response I'd say that you have not had much to do with my mother today, would that be right?"

Jessie gave a polite laugh. "Just when I got here this morning."

Donovan smiled and plucked a leaf from the tree branch near him.

"Linda said you own the restaurant. It's lunchtime.

Aren't you busy?" Jessie saw a lot of cars in the car park that she knew didn't belong to guests.

Donovan waved a hand in the air. "I own it, I don't work in it; I oversee it."

"You don't cook?"

"I can cook, but I've never cooked in the restaurant. My talents lie in other areas." He gestured toward the seat. "Mind if I sit?"

"Please do." Jessie moved over for him.

"We had another Amish girl here once."

"Yes, Linda told me that."

"Can't remember her name now. She was a lot older. I don't know why we call her a girl. More of a woman was what she was." Jessie followed Donovan's gaze and saw a man in a white chef's outfit waving at him. "Looks like I have to go and do some overseeing." He stood. "It was nice talking with you, Jessie."

She watched Donovan walk away. There was no one like him amongst anyone she knew. He was handsome, and his confidence made him even more attractive. His hair was dark brown, longish at the top and cut short at the back. He was well dressed in a light colored long-sleeved shirt, dark pants and black soft-leather shoes.

Was Donovan *Gott's* answer for her? She'd prayed for a husband and he came across her path. It wasn't unknown that an *Englischer* would leave their world behind them to join the community. Everything was possible with *Gott*. Her best friend, Olive, had met an *Englischer* who had just joined the community. Once Jessie would've ruled out *Englischers* as potential husbands, but Olive found a soon-to-be husband in Blake, so Jessie was now open to all possibilities. Even though

Blake and Olive weren't married yet, it was only a matter of time.

How could she find out more about Donovan? Linda seemed nice, but she was a no-nonsense person who would not take kindly to speaking about Mrs. Billings' son while they worked. Jessie did not have much experience with men although she knew enough to know that Donovan liked her; she could tell that in his eyes.

The afternoon passed swiftly, and Linda kept Jessie too busy to talk. It wasn't until the next day when Michelle was working that Jessie learned more about Donovan. Michelle had worked for Mrs. Billings for two years and had recently reduced her hours because she was expecting a baby.

As they stripped the sheets off the beds, Michelle told Jessie, "He was getting married late last year, but all of a sudden he called it off. No one found out why. Vanessa was the name of his fiancée—she was heartbroken. She even got a hammer and broke every window in his car." She leaned over as best she could and tucked the clean sheets precisely in at the corners.

Jessie's mouth dropped open that someone would do such a thing. "She must have been upset."

"He's always got a new girlfriend." She stood up straight. "I've just realized. I haven't seen him with a girl in some months. Hmm." She went back to making the bed. "Mrs. Billings said that you learn from me and Linda and then next week you're on your own. I reckon you should concentrate on what we're doing here and not think about the heartbreaker."

"I'm not." Jessie tried to concentrate, but could only think of Donovan and the fact that two women had warned her about him. Somehow, that only made him intriguing and she wanted to know more.

It was on the second day of her new job that Jessie saw Donovan again. She sat under the same tree for lunch and Donovan approached her.

"Two days, that's a record. I'm glad to see you're still here," he said.

She giggled. "Don't frighten me. I know Linda's been here for years, and Michelle's been here for two years."

"Yes, but they're two exceptional people: there have been many more who haven't made it."

"I hope I'm exceptional as well."

He looked at her carefully. "I think you might be."

Jessie giggled again, covering her mouth as she looked away. He sat down without waiting to be asked. She looked back at him and held his gaze while she experienced tingles rippling through her body. "I must go." She wrapped the remains of her sandwich.

"Why? You haven't even finished your lunch."

She stood up. "I'm not hungry now." There was something dangerous about him and that was exciting, but she knew she should stay away from him. She did just that and hurried away. A little voice nagged at her. If Olive had found her perfect man amongst the *Englisch*, might she too find her husband in the same manner?

Chapter Fifteen

Throughout that week, each day had been much like the first for Jessie, except she hadn't seen Donovan again. She regretted rushing away from him at lunch when she had. It would've been good to get to know him a little better.

On Saturday, she met Olive at the Coffee House.

"Jessie, there's a reason I asked you to come here early before the other girls get here." Olive Hesh lifted up her chin and tried to gain her best friend's attention.

Jessie sucked chocolate milkshake up through the straw and looked at Olive's concerned face. "I'm listening." Olive shook her head. "What? I am listening, but not if you're going to talk about Elijah again." Jessie knew that now Olive had a firm marriage prospect in Blake, she wanted the same security for her. But, Jessie wasn't so sure about Olive's brother. He always seemed so distant and aloof.

Olive giggled. "What do you think about him?"

Jessie rolled her eyes and pinched her straw between two fingers. There was no way she could tell Olive that Donovan had been occupying her thoughts. "I told you before I think he's very nice." She didn't want to tell Olive she'd once had a mad crush on Elijah, but he'd paid her no mind. If he hadn't been interested in her back then, he wouldn't be now.

"Nice? Nice in the way that you might be interested or nice in the way that he's a nice person, but you'd never like him?" Olive studied her friend carefully.

After a brief exhalation, Jessie pushed her milkshake away and looked up. "I don't know him that well."

"You do so know him. We've all grown up together."

"What I mean is he's quiet and doesn't say much." Jessie hoped she hadn't said too much. She'd known for a while that Olive wanted her to marry her *bruder*. Jessie had never told Olive she'd had to block him from her mind. That was a long time ago and those feelings had died.

"I know he's quiet, but he's a good person and would make a great husband. You two would be a perfect pair."

Jessie looked out the window of the coffee shop to see their three friends walking up the street to meet them. "Here they are."

Olive leaned back and looked out the window as well and waved to the three girls, Claire and Lucy and Amy.

"If he liked me, he'd do something about it." Jessie shrugged her shoulders. "It's clear he doesn't like me or he would've done something about it a long time ago. I don't know what you expect me to do."

Olive grabbed hold of her hand. "*Ach*, Jessie, is that all that's stopping you?"

Jessie frowned and shrugged. Their conversation came to an end when their three friends sat down. It was Saturday morning, and the five girls were all excited about their new jobs.

"I can't stay long today; I'm working at two." Lucy Fuller pushed some loose strands of dark hair back beneath her prayer *kapp*.

"How do you like your job, Lucy?" Olive asked.

"I love it, I'm working with the best people, and they have the most darling children."

"So, you're a nanny too, like Olive; I thought you got a job as a maid?" Jessie tapped her straw.

Lucy shook her head. "*Nee*, I only clean the house. They said they might give me a trial for the job when their nanny leaves in three months."

"What about your job, Jessie?" Claire asked.

Jessie could not contain the smile that broke out across her face. "I am working for a lady, Ramona Billings, who owns a B&B and her son has the large restaurant attached to it."

"I'd guess that the son is single and handsome going by that look on your face," Amy Yoder said.

"He is." Jessie giggled while out of the corner of her eye, she noticed Olive wasn't happy about her comment. "If *Gott* found Olive an *Englischer* who wanted to become Amish it could happen for me." She'd said it as a joke, but none of her friends laughed. In particular, Olive wasn't amused.

"All things are possible." Lucy's gaze traveled to Dan, the manager of the coffee shop, when he came to take their orders.

Jessie chose a coffee and a cupcake with chocolate frosting. After the other girls had ordered, they caught up on their latest news.

"How's Blake doing now that he's living in the community?" Amy asked Olive.

"He's slowly getting used to it. He's staying with the

Hiltys for six months before he takes the instructions." Olive giggled. "He said he thought he knew hard work until he'd done a day on the dairy farm."

"*Jah*, working on a dairy's the hardest work of all," Claire agreed.

"That worked out well for you, Olive," Amy said. "And, might he work in your parents' dairy when you marry?"

"*Nee*, definitely not. There's not even enough work there for all my brothers. Three can take care of it—*Dat* and two of my brothers—so there's not even work for my other three brothers." Olive giggled again. "Blake's counting down the days when he can finish up with the Hiltys and their farm."

"Were you in love with him as soon as you saw him?" Claire asked.

Everyone fell silent, looked at Olive and waited for her answer.

"I thought he was handsome, but he was an *Englischer*, so I never thought too much about him. He was also my boss. Anyway, there's a long way to go before we get married."

"*Jah*, but you know you will get married; you've found your *mann*," Jessie said.

"I hope so, but I have fearful thoughts he might change his mind and leave. His decision to join was quick. He might be a man who jumps into things without thinking them through and then regrets it. What if he changes his mind just as quick and leaves?"

"Don't look for things to go wrong, Olive. Enjoy the way *Gott's* blessed you," Claire said.

"I am, but—"

Dan, along with a waitress, brought their drinks and cakes to the table.

Jessie studied Olive's face; somehow, she'd changed. She'd gone from a shy girl to someone who was mature and self-assured. Even though she'd expressed some doubt about her fledgling relationship with Blake there was a quiet confidence about her, as someone would have who knew their life would be perfect. Within the year, Olive would marry Blake and be mother to his young son, Leo.

After lengthy conversations and two rounds of coffee and cake, they went their separate ways. Jessie had lingered outside the coffee shop and Olive walked back to her.

"You're not walking home, are you, Jessie?"

"I'll catch a taxi. My *vadder* brought me into town, but he said he couldn't wait for us to finish talking." Jessie giggled. "We've been three hours already. I guess he was right."

Olive linked arms with Jessie. "I'll drive you; I've got my buggy."

"Denke."

"Ach, we're going the wrong way. This way." Olive swung them both around on the sidewalk and they walked the other way.

Jessie knew she would have to put up with hearing more about Olive's *bruder* all the way home and she wasn't wrong.

As soon as the horse began walking, Olive began by saying, "You know he took someone else on a couple of buggy rides but that didn't last either. Someone besides Becca. She's married now anyway."

"By 'he' you mean Elijah?"

Olive giggled. *"Jah."*

"Jah, I heard that." Jessie looked out across the green fields as the horse clip-clopped rhythmically down the road. She wondered where she would be five years from now. Would she have her own house and be married, or would she be working at the B&B or working somewhere else?

"Jessie, you're not listening."

She turned to look into Olive's blue eyes. "What did you say?" Jessie was certain Olive hadn't said anything.

"I just want you to be happy, Jessie."

"I'm happy just as I am." Jessie looked at the road ahead, then asked, "Are you looking for another job now that Blake has joined the community?"

"I wanted to work and save some money to help us buy a home, but Blake won't hear of me working and said he's got plenty of money."

"Why ever not? Your *vadder* doesn't even mind you working."

"Blake said that he has more than enough money to buy us the best of everything."

Jessie stifled a giggle. "Why are you laughing?"

"He still sounds very *Englisch* saying 'the best of everything.'"

Olive smiled. "I'm teaching him. I told him I don't want fancy things. He had a hard time understanding, but he's learning quickly. From what he's told me, the *Englischers* strive to have nice things and be better than everyone else."

"That might be because a lot of them think that this life is all there is. They don't realize life is over like a snap of the fingers, and that eternity with *Gott* is forever. What use is storing up riches here?"

"*Jah,* that's right, we should store up riches in heaven. That's why I was worried about being too close to Blake in case he pulled me away from *Gott*. The bishop said going off the narrow way comes in subtle ways at first. We give in with the little things and before we know it we're off the path."

Olive was not being subtle; she was talking about her *bruder* again. Jessie knew Olive's *bruder* would not pull her away from *Gott*, but the handsome *Englischer*, Donovan, might. "You took a big risk with Blake and it worked for you. I don't see why something like that can't happen for me."

"Sounds like you want to get married." Olive looked over at Jessie waiting for an answer.

"Every girl wants to be married; I never said I didn't." Jessie frowned at Olive. "There's no point saying things to me about Elijah. If he'd ever liked me he would've done something about it by now. He's known me long enough."

"And like I said before, he's shy. I don't know why he's so quiet. He's handsome don't you think?" Olive sighed and looked at the road in front of her. "It's hard for me to tell since I'm his *schweschder*; I'm used to seeing him every day, and I don't look at him in that way anyhow." Olive glanced over again at Jessie and then gave her a sharp dig in the ribs.

"Ow. What did you do that for?"

"What's gotten into you lately, Jessie? You've gone all daydreamy, and you don't listen to me anymore."

Jessie scowled at Olive. "I'm thinking about things, that's all."

"About the boy who owns the restaurant; your boss's son?"

"He's not a boy he's a man. He's most likely in his late twenties, I'd guess."

"So that's a yes? You are thinking about him?"

Jessie lightly gnawed on a fingernail. "I guess."

Olive shook her head. "I see I'm getting nowhere. I'll talk about something else."

The rest of the drive home, Jessie was grateful that Olive spoke about subjects other than men.

When they got to Jessie's house, Jessie asked Olive to stay for a while, but Olive had chores to do for her *mudder*. Once Olive had driven away, Jessie decided she just had to speak to someone about Donovan. The perfect person was her *bruder* Mark. Conversations with him had become a lot easier with him in bed with a broken leg. Since it was Saturday afternoon, her parents were visiting friends.

"I'm home, Mark," she called out after she took her boots off in the laundry room.

"So am I, as always," came Mark's bored response from upstairs.

"Can I bring you something?"

"*Jah*, food; I'm starving."

"What do you want?"

"Anything. I could eat the leg off a chair about now."

"I'll fix you something." She heated up leftover pork and vegetables, and then took it upstairs. His face lighted up when she walked in the room with a tray of food.

"*Wunderbaar, denke.*"

"Did *Mamm* and *Dat* leave you here with no food?"

Mark broke off a piece of meat. "They left me food, but I ate it."

Jessie sat on the end of his bed. "Can I ask you something?"

Mark stopped chewing his food. "Is this about a boy again? You know I can't help you with those kinds of things. You should talk to one of your friends."

Jessie sighed. "I tried to talk to Olive, but she thinks Elijah is good for me, and she won't hear of anything else. I as good as told her I wasn't interested."

Mark finished his mouthful. "She could be right. I can see you two together. Although, he's quiet and you're *not* quiet; in fact, you're anything *but* quiet. I agree with her, you'd be perfect for each other. There, I've solved your problem already."

"Stop teasing. He's not interested either. I told Olive that. Why can't she see that for herself? And I told you about Blake, didn't I?"

"Several times, *jah*, so did *Mamm*. I'll meet him if this leg ever heals. No need to tell me about him again."

Despite his protests, Jessie continued, "Blake was an *Englischer* and if *Gott* made it happen for Olive, why can't He make it happen for me?"

Mark shrugged his shoulders with his eyes fixed on his food. "I don't know. Maybe you should speak to the bishop about something like that. Sounds like you might be heading toward dangerous ground with that thinking."

"How so?"

"You're determined to get me involved, aren't you?"

She untied the strings of her prayer *kapp*. "I'm interested in what you think because you are so smart. When you were working all the time I hardly got to speak to you except at night, and then everyone else was there."

"You really want to know what I think?" he asked between mouthfuls.

Jessie nodded her head vigorously.

"It's clear your eyes are on an *Englischer*." He gave his *schweschder* a knowing look, and then continued, "The closer you go to the edge of a cliff, the more chance you've got of falling off." Mark took his last portion of food and handed her the plate. "*Denke*, little *schweschder*. Now I need to rest." He laid his head back and closed his eyes.

Chapter Sixteen

The church gatherings were held every second Sunday and Mark and their parents set off in their buggy toward the Fishers' *haus* where the meeting was being hosted. The services always started early and carried through until late in the day. The evenings were less formal and mainly for the young, with the singings afterward.

As always, when she arrived, Jessie left her *family* and went in search of her four best friends. Olive caught her attention right away because she was waving a hand in the air. As Jessie got closer to her, she noticed a strange look on Olive's face. Staring at her trying to work out what was going on, she followed her gaze as it momentarily flicked off to one side. Jessie looked over to see that Olive was looking at Elijah.

Immediately Jessie feared Olive had said something to him. She didn't need these complications. "Olive, did you say something to Elijah about me?" she asked once she reached her friend.

"Not much really."

Jessie rolled her eyes. "You don't have to be my matchmaker. I'm perfectly all right as I am."

"Don't be so nervous and uptight. Everything always works out the way it's supposed to." Olive looked toward Elijah once more, so Jessie stood with her back to him. Olive then grabbed Jessie's hand. "The girls are saving seats for us."

They always sat on one of the back benches to get a good view of everyone. There was nothing the girls liked more than a good gossip especially when they could see the people they were whispering about. When the bishop got up to say a prayer, Jessie's eyes gravitated to the men's side of the room. It was always the men on one side and the women on the other.

Her eyes swept over all the men, and Jessie did not find one man who excited or intrigued her like Donovan did. He had the self-confidence that Elijah lacked.

Olive was right about Elijah being the logical choice of a husband for one of her friends. He was less appealing to Jessie because none of the other three friends considered him a potential suitor. In all of their conversations about men, no one had spoken of Elijah. *That could be because he was Olive's bruder*, Jessie thought, as she studied him from across the room. A loudly emphasized word from the bishop brought Jessie's attention back to his lengthy prayer.

Everyone sat down after the prayer, and the deacon, Amy's *vadder*, stood at the front of the room to read passages of Scripture from the Gospel of John. The deacon went on to explain how people should close their minds to evil and set their minds on *Gott*. The talks at the gatherings were always inspirational to Jessie.

After another long prayer, the first part of the gathering was over. Now it was time for the meal and the socializing. Jessie and her friends often helped with the food preparation, but Mrs. Fisher had told them that she had plenty of ladies to help this time.

Just as the evening singing was to begin, Jessie noticed Elijah walking toward her. He knew that she saw him, so she couldn't hurry away. She smiled at him.

"Hello, Jessie."

Jessie knew Olive was looking at both of them. "Hello," Jessie said.

"Jessie, I was wondering if I may take you home after the singing?"

A tiny spark of the interest she used to have in him was ignited. There was something warm about Elijah, and she heard herself say, *"Jah."* She looked into his blue-green eyes and his face softened into a smile.

"Gut. I'll see you after the singing."

Jessie nodded, and Elijah walked away just as Olive caught her by the arm. "What did he say?"

"He's taking me home after the singing."

A smile spread over Olive's face. "That's all I've been hoping for."

"You asked him to do this?"

"Perhaps I made a gentle suggestion, but he wouldn't have done it if he didn't want to."

Throughout the singing, Jessie got more and more nervous. She hadn't spoken to Elijah at any length for about two years. Back then, she had thought they were getting along fine, but he never did anything about it. Maybe she should have prompted him or dropped some hints that she liked him, but two years ago she considered that it was the man who should be the one to make the move. Now, it was a different story, but only because she was through with waiting. If she found a man she liked, she would do something about it.

The singing finished and Jessie hugged her friends goodbye, glad that Olive had kept quiet to her other friends about Elijah driving her home. Jessie looked around for Elijah and found him near his buggy.

"There you are. Set to go?" he asked.

"Jah." Jessie nodded.

Once they were both in the buggy, he smiled sweetly before he took the reins and clicked his horse forward. Things felt easy and comfortable with Elijah, even before they spoke.

"Olive tells me you've just started a new job."

"Jah, I've been there for a week now. It's the guest house out on the old road that leads to Drummonds Creek."

Elijah nodded. *"Jah,* I know the one. Enjoying it?"

"It's early days, but I think I will like it. Mrs. Billings, my boss, is very exact in the ways she wants things done."

He looked over at her and smiled again. "Lovely night, isn't it?"

Jessie looked up at the stars. "A million stars lighting up the night sky."

"Gott's designed them just for us to admire," Elijah said, looking upward from the topless buggy. He slowed his horse to a walk and looked over at her. *"Denke* for coming with me tonight, Jessie."

She wasn't sure what she should say, so she smiled and gave a little nod.

After a moment of silence, he said, "I've wanted to ask you on a buggy ride for some time, but I didn't know if you would. I mean, I guess I didn't want you to see me as foolish, and I would've felt embarrassed if you'd said no."

Nervousness forced Jessie's fingers to fiddle with the strings of her prayer *kapp*. Why hadn't he done this two years ago? "You've taken a girl out for a buggy ride before though, haven't you?"

"*Jah*, of course; not you though."

There was no doubt about it; from how he spoke and the way he looked at her, she knew he liked her and that was pleasing. After a few minutes of general conversation, they talked about their families. He ended up telling her funny stories about how forgetful his father was. His tales had her laughing more than she'd laughed in a long time. His sense of fun was one of the things she'd always liked about him. Not long after that, Elijah took her home—after she had agreed to go on another buggy ride with him.

When his horse and buggy were a distant sound, she ran up the stairs of the darkened house, grateful no one had waited up, and then she threw herself onto her bed and giggled. Olive might've been right; Elijah could be a match for her. *But what about Donovan?* One week ago, she'd had no prospect of a beau and today she had two.

Chapter Seventeen

Jessie woke the next morning after a restless night's sleep. She was taking a little longer to get ready for work making sure she wore her best dress and one of her best prayer *kapps*. As she drew a brush through her long wavy hair, she was mindful of what the bishop always said about a woman and her looks. A man should not look on the outside of a woman, but look within. Jessie was certain men were attracted by looks first, just as she and her friends talked about handsome men.

Her *vadder* drove her to work in the buggy, but she'd have to catch a taxi home. Just as Jessie said goodbye to her *vadder* and hurried down the long drive of the B&B, she noticed the building of the B&B and the restaurant were joined together. She'd thought they were separate. The B&B was old, and the restaurant was added later; possibly at the same time the renovations were done on the guest house. It was a clever addition.

This was the start of her second week and today she was on her own cleaning the rooms. She hoped she could meet the standards of Mrs. Billings. Before she reached the front doors, Jessie couldn't stop herself looking for Donovan's car. There it was; his sleek black car was in the parking lot. A rush of excitement ran through her body. He was back.

Jessie pulled her mind away from Donovan to concentrate on work, otherwise, she might not have a job. She knew she'd be the only maid working this morning. Linda was on a scheduled day off, and it wasn't Michelle's day to work.

She stacked the cart while wondering how to get it up the stairs. There was no way she could do it without Linda's help. Linda had been right; it was a silly place to have the cleaning room if they needed to drag the carts up and down the stairs every day. Jessie did not want to disturb Mrs. Billings, so she slipped into the restaurant to ask Donovan if she might borrow one of his workers to help lift the cart.

Being early, the front door of the restaurant was shut, so she went around to the back door. Just as she was about to knock, the door swung open, and Donovan walked out.

"Jessie." He looked her up and down.

"Hello, Donovan, I was coming to ask you if one of your workers might help me with the cart."

Donovan chuckled. "I was coming to do just that."

"Thank you."

"After you." Donovan gestured with a sweep of his hand toward the B&B.

She couldn't help but give a little giggle even though she felt silly straight away. She always did that when she was nervous. "I'm by myself today for the first time. I'm hoping I'll do a good job."

"You'll be fine."

"Do you have many people working for you in the

restaurant?" She hoped she hadn't asked him that before, or she'd feel stupid.

"I've got five full-time and some part-time workers. It varies as some leave and others arrive."

"You don't have the same people all the time?"

"My full-time staff are pretty stable, but I can't offer everyone full time and that's what most people around these parts want."

Jessie thought him remarkably young to have such a business.

Once the cart was at the top of the stairs, Donovan said, "It's not practical, I can't keep coming over and helping with this every day. It's ridiculous. I'll call some people for quotes on building something adjacent to the back door."

"Oh, I'm sorry, I didn't mean to be a nuisance."

Donovan smiled. "I didn't mean it like that. I don't mind helping, but I shouldn't have to. Do you see what I mean?"

"Yes."

"I'll leave you to it." Donovan gave her a smile, flashing a perfect set of white teeth.

Jessie found it hard not to smile when he was around. "Thanks again."

"I might see you at lunchtime."

"Okay." She stood at the top of the stairs and watched Donovan walk away. "Snap out of it, Jessie," she told herself in a whisper. She had to put all thoughts of him out of her mind and concentrate on being the best maid Mrs. Billings ever had. Just as she thought of her, Mrs. Billings appeared.

"There you are. I came to find you, and you weren't here."

"Sorry, Mrs. Billings, I had to ask for help with the cart. I can't get it up the stairs by myself. I wasn't gone long, and Donovan's just gone."

"That's quite all right. I know it's too hard for one person. I've been looking into locating the cleaning room to another part of the building." Mrs. Billings glanced down the stairs. "I've been thinking of making another bedroom out of the cleaning room and building an annex outside." Mrs. Billings tapped her chin. "Yes, that would work." She looked at Jessie and clapped her hands. "Hop to it. Those rooms will not clean themselves."

Jessie clasped the handle of the cart and pushed it to the first room wondering if she should've told her about Donovan getting quotes. *Nee, best not to mention a word.*

She knocked on the door of the first room and went in when no one answered. Once she was satisfied with a job well done, careful to do everything just as Linda had shown her, she moved into the next room. By lunchtime, she had all five rooms cleaned and she hurried out to her favorite seat in the garden hoping Donovan would join her.

When she had been there only five minutes, Donovan walked toward her. "Mind if I join you?"

"Please do."

"See." He sat down and then lifted up his sandwiches. "I had someone make these for me so I could come sit with you."

Jessie giggled.

"Do you have a boyfriend?"

With a raise of her eyebrows, she studied his face. He'd said it in a cheeky manner, so she found it hard to take offense at the prying question. "No, I don't."

"Why not? A pretty girl like you should have one." He moved so his shoulder touched hers.

He was getting way too close. "There aren't many men my age in the community."

"So, you'll have to look outside the community?"

She stared at the ground in front of her. "I'm not looking at all."

He leaned over to look directly into her face. "Really?"

Jessie narrowed her green eyes. "Yes."

Donovan straightened up and took a bite of his sandwich.

When he finished his mouthful, he said, "I like a strong independent woman."

She was pleased he wasn't looking at her when he spoke because she knew her cheeks were burning. As soon as Jessie ate her lunch, she made the excuse she wanted to do some things she'd forgotten, and she left him there.

"Finished lunch already, Jessie?" Mrs. Billings was standing just outside the laundry when she raced in the back door.

"Yes, I want to check on everything before I polish the silver this afternoon."

"No need; everything was adequate, but you should check as you go." Mrs. Billings folded her arms. "The silver's in the cleaning room and when you finish it you can go home."

"Thank you, Mrs. Billings." Jessie walked down the steps thinking she was in for an early finish, but when she got there, she saw nearly a day's worth of silver cleaning in front of her. She stifled a groan. She'd been warned Mrs. Billings expected a lot from her staff.

As Jessie polished the silver, she wondered whether Donovan was particularly interested in her or whether he was merely friendly. She ended up having to stay an hour beyond her finishing time to get all the silver cleaned.

When Jessie got home, she hurried up to her *bruder's* room and sat on the end of his bed. "Can I ask you something, Mark?"

"*Nee*, not if it's about a boy."

She pulled a sad face. "I've no one else to ask."

"Go on then." Mark flicked his eyes toward the ceiling and muttered something under his breath.

"Donovan, the boss's son, had lunch with me today in the garden. He said I was pretty and asked if I had a boyfriend."

Mark pushed himself higher in his bed. "He what?"

"Calm down; it wasn't as it sounds. I'll tell you exactly what he said and what happened." Jessie related the whole scene to Mark. "So, what do you think?"

"You should keep away from him. You need to make a decision. If you want to try the *Englisch* world then go on *rumspringa*, but you can't have one foot in the community and the other foot out."

Her eyebrows pinched together. "I'm asking you what you think that he's thinking. I don't want to go on *rumspringa*."

"I know exactly what he's thinking and you do too. Keep away from him."

Jessie jumped to her feet. "You don't even know

him. How could you know what he's thinking or what he wants?"

Mark threw his hands in the air and stuck his chin out. "Why'd you ask me then? You asked me, and I told you. It's as simple as that."

"He seems nice."

"He could be, Jessie, but you've got to protect yourself." He heaved an exasperated sigh. "Can't you find a man in the community?"

"Last night, Elijah brought me home from the singing. Did you know that?"

"Elijah Hesh?"

"Jah." She studied his reaction, and it seemed as though he approved of Elijah.

"He's a good man. He'd make a fine husband for you. Now forget about the *Englischer*. That is, if you want my advice."

"I do; your advice means a lot. I have no one else to talk with. The thing I've been wondering is why don't any of my friends like Elijah?"

"Would he be more appealing if one of them liked him?"

Jessie breathed out heavily. "It's not like that, exactly. I just wonder if they see some flaw I don't see."

Mark shook his head. "Why don't you talk with *Mamm*? You should speak to another woman about these things."

"Nee and don't you breathe a word to her! You know what she's like; she'd be straight over to his *mudder's haus*, and they'd be making wedding plans. You're the perfect person for me to talk with because you know how men think."

Mark lifted his leg slightly off the bed. "I should be

able to get about on crutches soon now the swelling and the pain have eased."

Selfishly, Jessie was a little disappointed; she liked having her *bruder's* attention without him away working or tired from a full day's work. "That's good. When do you get the crutches?"

"*Dat's* getting them for me tomorrow."

"It'll be a while before you can go back to work, won't it?"

"*Jah*, I won't be working for a few weeks, not 'til the leg mends."

Jessie smiled. "*Denke*, for giving me your words of wisdom. I'll bring some dinner up for you."

When she went to bed that night, all Jessie could think about were her *bruder's* words. Elijah, since he was in the community, and the only single man in her age range, would be the logical choice. The problem was now she wanted to find out more about Donovan.

Chapter Eighteen

The next morning was a humdrum day for Jessie, and Linda was back at work.

"This afternoon we have to clean the fireplaces in rooms one and two. They're the only rooms with fireplaces."

"I've never cleaned a fireplace before. My brother always does that at home."

"We'll do it together. There's a special way Mrs. Billings likes us to do them."

Jessie wasn't surprised. Mrs. Billings had a special way of doing everything. After they both pulled on cleaning gloves, Linda passed some equipment to Jessie, and they made their way to room one. First they spread newspaper from the fireplace to halfway across the room, and they were ready to begin.

"We take this spade, and scoop all the ash into the black, metal bucket." Linda leaned down and scooped. "When it's all out, we brush it clean. No need to do more, just brush."

"The people in here last night had a fire I see," Jessie said. "Yes, and so did the guests in room two, so we also have to restock the kindling and the firewood into that bucket there. We keep the firewood and the kindling in the locked room behind the restaurant."

"Do you want me to get it?" Jessie hoped she didn't sound too enthusiastic. If she went near the restaurant, she might see Donovan since she hadn't seen him at lunch time.

"In a minute. You try doing what I just did."

Linda stood up, and Jessie took over. "Do you think Mrs. Billings is pleased with my work?"

"You're still 'ere, aren't ya?"

Jessie looked up at Linda. "That means 'yes'?"

Linda nodded. "When we finish this one and the other fireplace, I'll go with you and show you where the firewood is kept."

An hour later, they had finished cleaning the fireplaces. They washed the black soot off themselves and Linda took hold of a key and they set off to get the firewood.

"He's not here today," Linda said, smiling at Jessie.

"What do you mean? Who's not here?"

"Donovan."

Jessie looked down at the ground as she continued to walk by Linda's side. "I didn't say anything."

"I can see your head swiveling about looking for him. Don't be embarrassed, you're not the first woman who's had a crush on him and I'm sure you won't be the last. He's had to drive his mother somewhere today. The day always goes more smoothly when she's not here checking up on everything."

Linda put the key in the lock, opened the door and they filled their cart with firewood and kindling. On the way back to the main building Linda said, "Since the old girl isn't 'ere, I'm leaving early. You can do the same thing if ya like. She won't ever find out; I won't be tellin' her." Linda laughed.

"No, I'll stay and work until my proper time."

They refilled the wicker baskets with wood in both of the two rooms, and then Linda left Jessie alone an hour before going-home time. At five o'clock, Jessie waited by the front fence for Olive to fetch her and take her for coffee as arranged. As usual, Olive was running late.

Jessie leaned down and plucked a wildflower by her feet and then she heard the low hum of a car. She looked up to see Donovan's car coming toward her. When his car turned into the driveway, he stopped next to her.

"Off home?"

"Yes, I'm waiting for a friend." Seeing no one else in the car with him, she said, "You were driving your mother somewhere today?"

"She had some appointments and won't be back until later tonight. Have there been problems here?"

"No, not at all."

His grin widened. "You missed me, didn't you?"

"I noticed you weren't around." Jessie looked up when she heard the clip-clop of horse's hooves. "Here's my friend now."

Donovan ignored her words. "I've been thinking about you, Jessie. In fact, I can't get you out of my mind."

Jessie looked at him thinking he might be joking. When she saw he was serious, she swallowed hard.

He glanced around at the advancing buggy, and looked back at Jessie. "Would it be out of the question for you to have dinner with me one night? I know you have rules and everything. Do the rules forbid two people having a meal together?"

Her eyes were locked onto his and she knew from the sound of the hooves that the buggy was close. She also knew that she would get a hundred and one questions from Olive about the man in the car. "Can I talk to you tomorrow? I have to go." Jessie walked away.

"I'll meet you at lunchtime in the garden," he called after her.

She called over her shoulder, "Okay."

Just as she knew she would, Olive questioned her as soon as she climbed into the buggy. "Who's that in the car?"

Jessie looked at Donovan's car zooming up the driveway. "The boss's son. He owns the restaurant."

"Oh, that's him?"

Jessie knew she would have to change the subject. "How was your day?"

"Fine, it was fine."

"Well, what did you do now that you're unofficially betrothed and officially unemployed, or retired, or something?" Jessie was talking fast to keep the conversation away from Donovan.

"I'm working on a quilt. I've joined my *mudder's* quilting group."

Jessie laughed. "Just like an old married lady."

"*Jah*, I will be one soon. But the bishop said we couldn't get married for six months because he's got to adjust to the community and also get baptized, of course."

"I suppose you never expected to find someone outside the community."

"*Nee.*" Olive shook her head. "I never even thought of it."

* * *

When the girls arrived at their coffee shop, they were pleased their usual table was free.

Dan met them at the door. "Hello, girls. You're a little late today."

"You're not closing, are you?" Olive asked.

"*Nee*, we're open for dinners now; light dinners. And will the others be joining you?"

"It's just us today." Jessie knew that Dan liked Lucy, and it was clear from his face that he was trying to hide his disappointment.

"Do you know what you want?" Dan asked.

Jessie was a little hungry, but she knew her *mudder* would have a big meal waiting for her. She looked in the glass display case at all the cakes. There was an array of sweet cakes and cookies, but she did not want anything too sweet. It was a choice of banana bread or gingerbread. "The gingerbread looks good. Can you toast that?"

"We toast it and you can have it with butter." After he spoke, Dan waited politely for the two girls to make a decision.

"I'll have gingerbread and a cappuccino." Jessie turned to Olive. "What are you having?"

"Oh, that looks good."

Jessie read the label on what Olive had been pointing to. It was a banana cupcake with chocolate ganache. "Have one then."

"Okay, I'll have one of those and a black coffee, thanks, Dan."

"Black today?"

"Yes, for a change," Olive answered.

The girls walked to their usual table and sat down.

"Now that we're alone, tell me how things went with Elijah," Olive said.

Jessie wished she could speak to Olive and ask her opinion of the two men, but one was Olive's *bruder,* so she was hardly an impartial person to speak with. "We had a nice talk, and he's pleasant."

"He's good-looking too. Girls tell me that all the time."

Jessie smiled. "*Jah,* he is."

Olive wriggled in her seat. "Jessie, you seem to be holding something back from me; what is it? We've always told each other everything."

Taking a deep breath, Jessie said, "It's just that I've met someone."

Olive's nose wrinkled and her eyebrows drew close together. "You have? Where?"

"Where I work."

"Not that *Englischer* I saw you speaking with when I arrived? You said he is the boss's son—the same one you were telling the girls about the other day?"

"*Jah,* that's the one. I don't know him very well. I've spoken to him a few times in the past week."

"What's so good about him?"

"The way he makes me feel. He's confident, and he's got that restaurant with people working for him and he's so young. That's impressive."

Dan interrupted them when he brought their coffees and food. "There you go, ladies. Enjoy."

"Thanks, Dan," they both said, and laughed.

Olive carefully lifted her cupcake out of the paper holder. "I mean, you don't know this man, as you said. He could be putting on a good act."

"*Nee*, I've only just met him but he seems nice. I like him."

"And you like Elijah as well?"

"There's something I never told you about Elijah."

Olive leaned back. "What?"

"I liked him two years ago and nothing happened, and I doubt anything will."

Olive's eyes grew wide, and then she quickly bit into her cake. As she chewed, she frowned at Jessie. When she had swallowed, she said, "You didn't tell me that. When was that?"

"We used to talk a little at the volleyball games and I liked him from that point. Then I saw a girl in his buggy, Andrea, so I knew he didn't like me. I put him out of my mind."

Olive nodded. "I remember her. They didn't last."

Jessie shrugged. "*Jah*, well. I don't know. He never seemed interested, so there was nothing I could do about it."

"You should have said something to me."

"*Nee*. I couldn't say anything. I didn't want him to like me because I liked him. Do you see what I mean?"

"*Nee.*" Olive shook her head.

Jessie lunged and grabbed her arm. "Don't dare breathe one word of this to him."

"Why not?"

"*Nee*, please, just don't say one word."

Olive narrowed her eyes. "Okay, I won't say anything, but you're being senseless."

"Me? He's the one who acted as though he liked me and then nothing. He never did anything about it. I'm not going to ask him on a buggy ride or ask him to the coffee shop. I'm just not."

"I'm sure he would've had a reason."

"*Jah*, probably the reason was that he didn't like me enough." Jessie shook her head. "I'd rather not know."

"*Nee*, I can tell he likes you. Don't ruin it by thoughts of that *Englischer*."

Jessie slumped back in her seat. "Things worked out for you when you fell in love with Blake and now he's joined the community. Don't forget he was an *Englischer*."

Olive smiled. "I'm not forgetting."

"This is the happiest I've ever seen you. If *Gott* found an *Englischer* for you, I don't have to choose from within the confines of the community, do I?"

"Well, probably not, but then there's Elijah."

"Claire, Lucy or Amy haven't said anything about liking him, so they can't find him appealing." Jessie held her breath as soon as the words tumbled out of her mouth, wishing she could take them back. From Olive's expression, the words had offended. Jessie lowered her head and spread the butter onto her hot toasted gingerbread.

"*Ach*, I was just trying to be helpful. I know what a good man he is. He's perfect for you. He's quiet by nature and you're outgoing, so you'd balance each other." Olive sipped her coffee.

"I'm sorry. I didn't mean it like that. I just meant that—well you can't push these things, they just happen."

"I know what you're saying, but how often does a man, or anyone, join the community? You're taking a big risk by liking the *Englischer* hoping he'll convert."

"Funny you would say that—you of all people. I thought you'd be the one to understand."

Olive shook her head. "I didn't chase Blake."

"Do you think I'm chasing Donovan?" Jessie scratched her neck.

"That's what it looked like. You were leaning over the car smiling at him."

Jessie was upset by Olive's words. "I was just being nice."

"You know what I mean. You smiled and fluttered your eyelashes at him; flirting with him. I could tell you were."

"I wasn't doing it on purpose. I'd never do that." Jessie didn't want to be angry with her best friend. She picked up her spoon and stirred the chocolate sprinkles of her cappuccino, mixing it in with the froth.

"That's what I saw." Olive shrugged.

Jessie nodded. "Is it so important that I like your *bruder*?"

"You're my dearest friend, Jessie. I want you to be as happy as I am. I thought I was happy until I met Blake, and now I feel like I need a new word that describes something far beyond happy." Olive's eyes sparkled as she spoke. "I don't want to be a meddler. I'll leave you alone to make your own decision. I hope it's my *bruder*, but if it's not, I hope it's someone who makes you happy. For all your life."

After the girls changed the subject, all ill feeling between them was forgotten. Olive drove Jessie back to her *haus*. "Stay for dinner, Olive?"

"*Jah*, that would be nice. I'm not expected back at any particular time."

Once they tied up the horse and gave him some

water, the girls hurried into the *haus*. Mark was trying out his crutches.

"Hello, Olive."

"Hi, Mark."

Jessie's *mudder* appeared in the living room. "You staying for dinner, Olive?"

"*Jah* if that's all right."

Jessie's *mudder* ushered the two girls into the kitchen to help with the last of the dinner preparations and to set the table.

During dinner, Mark, who was out of his bedroom the first time in weeks, asked Olive questions about Elijah. Jessie noticed that her *mudder* looked up from her food and sat straight in her chair at the mention of Elijah's name.

Jessie did her best to talk about other things to distract her mother hoping *Mamm* would not try to match the two of them together.

Chapter Nineteen

That night, Jessie couldn't sleep. Thoughts whirled through her head. Olive had been right about not many people joining the community. Then she worried that Donovan might've thought she was flirting with him, as it had appeared so to Olive. Perhaps she'd encouraged him too much and that was why he'd asked her out to dinner.

The next morning at work, lack of sleep made Jessie feel sick, and there was no sign of Donovan. She and Linda struggled to lift the carts upstairs before cleaning the rooms, and back down the stairs when they'd finished. Jessie wondered how Linda had put up with that for so many years.

At lunchtime, Jessie took her chicken sandwiches outdoors to eat out on her favorite seat under the tree in the middle of the grounds. She wasn't there long before Donovan approached.

Happiness flooded through her at the sight of him. "Hello, I didn't think you were coming today."

Smiling a secretive smile, he sat beside her. "Have

you thought more about what I asked you, about coming out with me one night?"

"I… I don't think I can."

"I don't think I can," he repeated. "I hear hesitation. That means you want to, but you think you shouldn't. Is that right?"

Jessie put her sandwich down into her lap. "Something like that."

"I'm very persistent, you should know. I won't give up."

It pleased her to hear him say that; she wanted to go to dinner with him. It was hard to say no, but she had to listen to her *bruder*. Maybe she could wait for time to pass and get to know him a little better. There was no rush.

"Penny for your thoughts."

She looked up at the sky, and pulled out the first thing that came into her mind. "Just thinking about my brother."

"What about him?"

"Nothing really; he's just got a broken leg. Some weeks ago, he fell off the roof and got a very bad break. He's on crutches now. It was getting better, but he put too much weight on it too soon and broke it again."

"Ouch, sounds painful."

"He's tough." Jessie bit into her sandwich wondering why she hadn't found something—anything—more interesting to talk about. "Do you have any brothers or sisters?"

"No. Once mother had me, she decided she couldn't improve on perfection." He chuckled, but Jessie didn't laugh. "I'm joking. It was a bad joke, I know."

"Oh." Jessie laughed then, but it had sounded like

something Mrs. Billings might've really said. "Your mother does like things just so."

"I pretty much keep out of her way as much as I can."

"She must be very proud of you having your own restaurant."

"She never says so. I don't need her approval. I've always been interested in business. I've also got a coffee shop in town I'm considering franchising."

"What does that mean?"

"The best way I can explain franchising is like this: It's where you take one business and duplicate it elsewhere. I could have coffee shops all over the country. The difference is that other people would own them and manage them. I would sell them the business model and help them with knowledge of how to run it. Every aspect of the business would have a particular way it should be run to keep them the same. All the procedures would be written in the business manual. I'll make money selling the businesses, and I'll collect the ongoing franchise fees."

"That sounds like a good idea. You're a detail person, just like your mother."

"A detail person—yes. Like my mother—no." Jessie giggled.

"Anyway, that's what's keeping me busy these days. I'm working on getting the coffee shop in ship-shape form so it can be my flagship store." He took a bite of his sandwich.

"Sounds as though you have a lot of plans."

When he'd finished chewing and had swallowed, he said, "I'm going places. I've always had a drive to succeed. I sold lemonade when I was seven, I had a paper route when I was eleven, and I had a thriving Internet business when I was fifteen, which I sold to buy the restaurant. Out of the money I made from the restaurant, I bought the coffee shop."

Jessie knew he didn't own the Coffee House, where she and her friends went. Dan's parents owned that. More than likely it was one of the newer upmarket cafés. She didn't choose to ask which one it was.

"What about you, Jessie? What do you see in your future?"

"My future is pretty much the same as every Amish woman. Family is very important to us, and I'd love to have a lot of children."

"So would I."

Jessie looked at him. "You would?"

He dug her in the ribs. "Don't look so surprised."

"Sorry, it's just that I didn't think you would want a family and children and all that."

Donovan tipped his head back. "All I ever wanted when I was a child was a brother or a sister. I nagged my mother for years to have another child, and she said it would ruin her figure. I'd never have just one child, not after how it was for me growing up."

Jessie giggled.

Donovan inched closer to her. "Don't laugh, it's true."

"How many would you have?" Jessie looked at him as he looked straight ahead.

"I'd say the ideal number would be four. Two boys and two girls would be about right." He turned to her and smiled.

Jessie's stomach flip-flopped and she had to look away.

Chapter Twenty

When Jessie's father drove her home, she saw a buggy parked at their *haus*. "Is that Elijah's buggy?"

"*Jah*, his *mudder* sent him over with whoopie pies."

Jessie wondered if his *mudder* had sent him over with the whoopie pies or whether it was Olive's idea.

"He's staying for dinner."

"He is?"

Her *vadder* nodded.

Mr. Miller stopped the buggy in front of the house so Jessie could walk straight in. When she opened the door, she saw her *bruder,* Mark, and Elijah sitting in the living room.

"Hello, you two."

Elijah rose to his feet. "Hello, Jessie."

"If you'll excuse me, I'll need to clean up. I've had a busy day." Jessie hurried up the stairs and once she was in her bedroom, she closed the door. She sat on her bed and lay down. She wasn't prepared to see Elijah today. Had their *mudders* gotten together and were they trying to match them? Or, was it Olive? Was her friend the one who'd sent him over with the whoopie pies?

After Jessie had washed her face and changed her clothes, she went downstairs to help her *mudder* with dinner. She was glad her *bruder* was entertaining Elijah in conversation when she walked past them on her way to the kitchen. "What can I do to help, *Mamm*?"

Her *mudder* swung around to face her. "*Nee*, you go out to Elijah. I'm about done in here and the table is ready."

Jessie looked at the table wondering how she could help. "Go on, off with you." Her mother walked toward her making shooing motions with her hands.

Jessie swallowed hard and walked out to their guest.

As she approached the couch, her *bruder* leaned forward. "If you'll excuse me, Elijah, I've got a few things to attend to before dinner."

"Certainly."

Her brother carefully pushed himself up off the couch while hanging onto the crutches.

"Do you need help?" Elijah offered.

"*Nee*, I'm fine."

Jessie shot her brother a glare before she sat with Elijah. Mark smiled at her, got his crutches positioned and gave her a wink as he left the room.

"How was your day at your new job, Jessie?"

All Jessie could remember of her day was sitting in the garden while she and Donovan spoke on how many children they'd have. "It was a *wunderbaar* day."

Elijah smiled, and Jessie had to admit to herself that he was handsome.

"It must be *gut* to have work that you enjoy so much."

Jessie raised her eyebrows. "You enjoy working on the farm, don't you?"

"Not so much. I'm going to learn construction work with my *onkel*."

"Building houses and such?"

Elijah nodded.

While she sat and talked with Elijah, she couldn't help comparing him to Donovan. Donovan was better looking, more confident, but they were equally hardworking. Elijah was the more obvious choice given that he was Amish, but she would not rule Donovan out just yet. He was the one who made her heart race and her body tingle.

"Would you come for a buggy ride with me after dinner? It seems like it's going to be a nice night."

Jessie would have preferred her whole *familye* not know when she went on a buggy ride. They would ask her a ton of questions, such as, *how was it, do you like him, does he like you, are you going to get married?* She groaned inwardly at the thought of having to answer those types of questions. "*Jah*, I'd like that." She figured she'd give him a fair chance since a relationship with him made sense.

When dinner was over, they retired to the living room. Jessie's *mudder* would not even allow her to help clean up. Elijah must have had a word with Jessie's *vadder* because when she came out of the kitchen, Elijah stood before her, and he said in a low voice, "Let's go."

She nodded and in two minutes they were in his buggy. His sprightly bay horse took off at quite a pace with his head held high.

"I hope you don't mind me coming tonight," Elijah said.

"*Nee*, of course I don't mind. It was nice to see you." He glanced over at Jessie. "Really?"

She nodded.

"Truth is, I couldn't stop thinking about you all day."

She frowned at him. "Your *mudder* didn't send you over?"

Elijah laughed. "*Nee*, it was my idea and my *mudder* baked the whoopie pies for me to bring."

"Ah, I thought it might've been Olive's idea."

"Olive?"

"*Jah.* I think she'd be happy if the two of us became a couple."

"She's never mentioned anything of the kind. So, she's said that to you?"

"Once, or maybe twice."

He took his eyes from Jessie and looked back at the road. "I don't want you to feel pressured. I shouldn't have come tonight. I wouldn't have if I'd known that."

Jessie searched for something to say, but what could she say without giving him hope? She didn't want him to be disappointed. "Don't say that, it was nice to see you again." Out of the corner of her eye, she looked at his profile. He had handsome, angular features and a straight nose, which was neither too big nor too small. He glanced over at her once more, and she looked away and silence followed. Again, she searched for something to say. "I was talking to someone today who was an only child; he said that it was awful."

"*Jah*, I imagine that would be awful."

"That's the good thing about being in the community though. There's always someone. If I hadn't any siblings, it wouldn't have mattered because I've got Olive, Lucy, Amy and Claire who are just like my sisters, except we don't have the same parents."

"I couldn't imagine not being in the community, could you?"

Jessie shook her head. "*Nee*, I couldn't even go on *rumspringa*. I'd miss my *familye* too much. You didn't go on *rumspringa*, did you?"

"*Nee*, I didn't. I couldn't leave the community." Elijah chuckled. "Jessie, I'm a quiet man and I find it hard to speak to people."

He looked away from the road and looked at her; she thought he looked nearly as handsome as Donovan.

Elijah continued, "What I'm trying to say, in my awkward way, is I'd like to see more of you than Sundays at the gatherings."

Put on the spot, she searched her mind for an intelligent response. If she said "yes" then they would soon court and she would be expected to marry him after a suitable time. If she said "no" she knew he would be too shy to ask again, and she would lose him forever. "I'd like that." That was the only thing she could say, and at that moment, she wanted to see where things between them would go. She considered him genuine, and he was giving her the same warm feelings that she had with Donovan.

From the smile on his face, Jessie knew that she had made the right decision. Her eyes fell from his face to his hands. They were large and strong as they loosely held the reins. It felt good to have two men interested in her.

Elijah relaxed when Jessie agreed to see more of him. He stopped the buggy, and they talked for some time. "Let's go for a walk."

"Okay," she agreed. The moon was high in the sky, and tonight it shone with luminous gold light.

"I love looking at all the stars, especially on a night like this."

"They're beautiful, aren't they?" Jessie turned her head slowly to put the moon behind her and face the stars.

"It makes me wonder why *Gott* bothers so much with us. The world is so large, and we are so small." He chuckled a little. "To think that He created everyone and everything; I do wonder why He made people."

"I never really thought of it."

"I think of things like that all the time. Just think of a leaf and how it has all the tiny veins and patterns, and that's just in one small leaf. I wonder why He would take time to put designs into things that might never be seen." He looked up to the sky. "Then you look at the stars and wonder why He put them there. Was it for us to enjoy? Maybe to prove to us that there's something bigger than we are. The Scripture says we see His handiwork in the stars."

Jessie looked away up at the stars again. It was a beautiful moment, and she was glad she was with Elijah.

Elijah looked at her and smiled. "Now you know what things run through my mind."

"I like it. It's good to think deeply about things and not just take everything around us for granted."

"Well, mostly I think of work because that's what I do nearly every day." After a silence, he asked, "What things do you think of?"

"I think of what it'll be like to have *kinner*." Jessie giggled.

"I think you'd make a *gut mudder*, Jessie."

"You do?"

He nodded. "*Jah*, you're straightforward and speak your mind. I don't think you'd put up with nonsense. You'd be firm and fair."

Jessie smiled and looked away. She was surprised he knew her so well. Lately though, she had not been straightforward, and she struggled with speaking her mind.

"I can see you with many *kinner*," he added.

"What about you, do you want a lot?" Jessie asked.

"*Ach, jah*, about a dozen or even more."

Jessie giggled. "More than a dozen? That's a lot."

"*Kinner* make a happy home. That's what life's all about—*familye* and bringing them up to know *Gott*."

Jessie nodded and then looked up into his eyes, liking him being a good six inches taller.

He stepped a little closer and his gaze lowered to her lips before he cleared his throat. "It's getting late; we should head back." She wanted to hear him speak some more and didn't move. He lightly touched her shoulders and turned her to face the buggy. "Let's go," he said.

Moments later, they were back at Jessie's *haus*. Elijah pulled the horse to a halt by the front door. "*Denke* for coming out with me tonight."

"I really enjoyed it." She'd enjoyed his company more than she had thought she would. "I'll see you again soon."

"I hope so."

She jumped out of the buggy and hurried to her house. Everyone was in bed when Jessie crept through the front door. There was a lone gas light on in the living room. She lit the gas lantern that someone had left out for her, doused the light and quietly made her way up the stairs to her room. Thankfully, she did not have to talk to anyone or answer any questions about her time with Elijah.

Once she was settled in bed, she closed her eyes and images of Elijah drifted through her mind. She could see herself married to him. She was sure Olive had been behind him being there tonight, even though Elijah had said it was his idea.

Pushing her annoyance at Olive aside, Jessie pulled the sheet over her head and imagined what it would be like to be in Elijah's strong arms. It was weird that when she was with Elijah she liked him, but when she was with Donovan she liked him. Right now, Donovan was a distant memory but how would she feel when she saw him again?

Chapter Twenty-One

Jessie woke the next morning pleased to have a good sleep, but it was way too early to wake. The sun had not even appeared on the horizon. She took a deep breath of fresh air as it breezed through the partially open window. Turning over, she folded her pillow under her head. Elijah's words and thoughts were in her mind from the previous night. He was a serious man of *Gott* who wanted the same things as she did. Elijah would make her a *gut* husband.

Donovan was exciting and interesting. He was also hardworking and had said he wanted many children, so those were things in his favor.

There was only one thing she could do before she made any further commitments either way. She would have to get to know Donovan a little more. Maybe Donovan was a Christian or was open to know about *Gott*. She closed her eyes tightly. *Nee, maybe Olive was right. I shouldn't let an* Englischer *sidetrack me. I have a* gut *Amish man interested in me, so I should block out all thoughts of Donovan and concentrate on Elijah. That would be the right thing to do.*

"You'll be late if you don't wake up now."

Jessie woke with a start at the sound of her *mudder's* voice. The sun was well over the horizon, she saw when she looked out the window. She'd drifted off to sleep again. "I'm coming, *Mamm*."

"Breakfast is on the table."

"Denke," she called to her *mudder* from the bedroom. "I'll be a couple of minutes." She'd gone to bed without braiding her hair and now it was full of tangles. With her fingers, she worked out the worst tangles. Then, with broad strokes, she dragged a brush through her hair, braided it and pinned it to sit nicely under her prayer *kapp*. Once she'd pulled on her lemon-colored dress and her apron, she secured her *kapp*. From the aroma wafting up the stairs, she knew her *mother's* pan-fried scrapple was for breakfast.

Before she went downstairs, she stuck her head around her *bruder's* bedroom doorway. "I've got a lot to tell you, but I'm late for work. I'll see you when I get home." Her *bruder* grimaced. She knew he didn't want to hear everything that was going on in her life, but his advice was always exactly what she needed. Her head was in such a muddle, now that she had two romantic prospects after having none for so long.

No sooner had she sat down and started to eat *Mamm* wagged a finger at her. *"Dat's* got the buggy waiting. Don't eat too fast, or you'll get a pain in your belly."

Jessie nodded as she cut a small piece of scrapple. Then her mother placed a cup of not-too-hot coffee in front of her. *"Denke, Mamm."*

"How was your buggy ride with Elijah?" Her mother sat next to her and peered into her face as though she was trying to catch something in her expression.

Since Jessie had a mouthful, she could only nod. When she had swallowed, she took a large mouthful of coffee. "Got to go, *Mamm*." She kissed her mother goodbye and raced out the door before her mother had a chance to ask again.

How could she tell her mother how she felt when she wasn't sure herself? She certainly could not tell her about Donovan and let her know she had any sort of feelings for an *Englischer. Mamm* would surely faint if she heard that. No, the only person she could share that with was her *bruder*. He was more open to things—reacted more calmly—since he had some friends who'd been on *rumspringa*.

The journey to the B&B was quiet since her *vadder* was not much of a talker. He would not ask her questions like her *mudder* had.

"There you are." *Dat* stopped the buggy in front of the long driveway.

"*Denke*. Can you collect me, or should I get a taxi?"

"*Nee*, I'll come get you."

Jessie exchanged smiles with her *vadder* and hurried inside the B&B. She looked up at the clock on the wall of the reception area absolutely horrified to see she was ten minutes late.

"Morning, Jessie."

"Morning, Yvonne," she said to the receptionist as she hurried past. When she raced down the stairs, she saw Donovan. "Donovan."

He glanced at his watch. "Here you are."

"Yeah, I know. I'm so sorry I'm late. It won't happen again." She had no good excuse.

"That's fine. Linda's twisted her ankle, though, so it'll be just you for the next few days. Can you handle it?"

"Yes, I can. I will. Where's your mother?"

"She's away too."

"Oh. She didn't say anything."

"It was all last minute. Anyway, I'm here to help you get the cart up the stairs."

Jessie tried to steady her breathing. "Thank you, that was kind of you to remember me."

He wheeled the cart to the bottom of the steps.

"Wait; I need to fill it first." Jessie spun around and put all the necessary things in the cart.

He leaned against the wall and folded his arms while watching her gather the cleaning equipment. "Since you won't agree to dinner, what about lunch? Lunch today with me?"

Jessie spun around to face him. "I'm not sure."

"You normally have lunch at one. I'll meet you right here at one. It'll just be a quick lunch, not a date or anything, so you needn't look so worried."

"Not a date?"

"Definitely not! You'll be doing me a favor, and you'll find out why when we're at lunch."

She relaxed her shoulders. *If it wasn't a date it might be all right,* she considered. She was still conflicted, however, since she'd made a commitment to Elijah. "Okay, I'll meet you here at one."

Donovan left her at the top of the stairs once he'd helped her with the cart. All was quiet at work with Linda and Mrs. Billings gone. Only three groups of people had stayed overnight. Two had checked out and the others were there for a longer stay. From the noise in the first room, the people were still in there, so Jessie began with one of the vacated rooms at the other end of the hallway.

Jessie cleaned each of the rooms as fast as she could while constantly trying to remember exactly how Linda said that Mrs. Billings wanted things done. When one o'clock came, Donovan found her.

"Let's go."

She washed her hands and took off her work apron while he waited. Then she walked with him to his car. With a flourish, he opened the door for her and she slipped into the low leather seat. She'd only ever ridden in taxis, never in a car that was this fancy; she knew it must have cost a lot of money.

Once he'd slipped into the seat next to her, he said, "I hope you're hungry."

"A little bit."

"We're going to check out my opposition."

"Oh, that's the favor?"

"Exactly. I haven't been there for a long time. I want to see what they're up to. I don't think they'll know me." Donovan chuckled. "It's just five minutes up the road. Don't worry. I'll get you back to work on time, more or less."

"Is there a B&B next to the restaurant we're going to?"

He laughed. "No, it's a restored farmhouse. They've had excellent reviews. I'd like to see firsthand what I'm up against."

She looked at Donovan's hands on the steering wheel just as she had studied Elijah's hands as he held the reins. Donovan's hands were masculine as well but lacked the work-hardened appearance of Elijah's. Now, at lunch, was her chance to learn more about Donovan.

"Here we are."

Jessie looked out the window at the building which appeared to be made out of stone. "It looks very old."

"It's one of the oldest houses around."

They were shown to a table in a room almost aglow with fancy white starched tablecloths, shining silverware and crystal glasses. Once the waitress left, Jessie looked across at Donovan. "It's nice."

"You haven't been to my restaurant, have you?"

"No, I've just been to the back door." In her heart, she had secretly wanted him to take her out to a special lunch. That would've been romantic and exciting. Maybe he was too occupied with work to focus on a relationship.

It was odd that he was spying. Why did he need to do that? Her *vadder* was a farmer and never spied on neighboring farms.

"Ha, look at this." He picked up the menu. "They say they only use organically grown food; no fertilizers are used, and no hormones, antibiotics or steroids in their grass-fed beef. The water they use here is filtered, and all the food is local. The fish are even caught locally." He laughed. "They're trying to make out they support the local community."

"You don't believe what they say?"

"No, of course not; it sounds like something I'd say. In fact, it's a good idea; I might put something like that on my menu."

"Would it be true?"

Donovan threw his head back and laughed. "My father always used to say *don't let the truth get in the way of a good story.*"

Jessie could scarcely believe her ears. "Is this another one of your jokes?"

His shoulders dropped, and he tipped his head to the side. "Do you really think it matters whether people drink filtered water or whether their meat is free of hormones?"

"I don't know, but if that's what you say it is, then that's what it should be. Otherwise, you're a deceiver and wouldn't there be a law against it?"

He shrugged his shoulders, looked back at the menu, and murmured, "It's just business."

Jessie could not keep quiet. "No, it's not just business. If you do business like that, you'll not have a business for long because no one will trust you."

He looked up and laughed. "Look at your face. Don't take everything so seriously, Jessie."

"Don't you take your business seriously?"

"I do." He looked down at the menu for a moment. "Come on, do you really believe they use one hundred percent organic food? No, they would get whatever they could at the cheapest possible price to maximize their profit. That's what any business owner who was worth anything would do."

"I don't agree."

"They even say their coffee is organic and fair trade."

"Yes, and the coffee shop where I go with my friends has that kind of coffee, and it doesn't cost any extra."

Donovan frowned at her. "Don't be so sensitive, Jessie."

Chapter Twenty-Two

They hadn't even ordered their food and Jessie had already learned that Donovan was unscrupulous. *He could change,* she figured. *Everyone deserves a chance. Everyone has done wrong things.* She did her best to overlook his previous comments and was determined to find some good in this man who made her skin tingle and her heart race. Even though warning bells were sounding loud and clear, she didn't want to end up marrying Elijah and be left wondering if something could've worked between her and Donovan.

"My restaurant is much the same as this one because I modeled mine from it." He scratched his chin. "I might poach their head chef. Mine's starting to be unreliable."

"You mean, you'll get their chef to work for you?"

"Of course, if he's any good."

Jessie was too nervous to eat much, so she looked down the menu trying to find something light. "I might have the roasted pumpkin salad."

He craned his neck to see her menu. "Where's that?"

"About halfway down."

"Ah, comes with poached beetroot, goat feta, apple

and pear vinaigrette tossed with lettuce. Interesting combination."

"What looks good to you?"

"I'll try their surf and turf. You can tell a lot about a chef by how he cooks the steak. I can also see if he's fussy about using fresh seafood. I can tell whether the seafood's fresh or not."

"They wouldn't use seafood that's not fresh would they?"

"Some use frozen seafood rather than fresh, but I can taste the difference. If the head chef doesn't care too much, he'd use frozen."

Jessie nodded and closed the menu.

Donovan picked up the wine list. "Shall we order a bottle of wine?"

"No, I don't normally drink, and I've got to go back to work, remember?"

"Well, you don't really have to go back to work with Linda and my mother not being there. I'll have a word with Yvonne. She'll keep quiet."

Jessie leaned back. "I couldn't do that."

Donovan laughed. "I can see I've got to teach you a few things about life."

The waiter came to take their order, interrupting their conversation.

When the waiter left, Jessie asked, "You will have me back at work on time, won't you? I can take an hour for lunch if I work half an hour later, but generally I only take half an hour for lunch."

He reached over and took hold of Jessie's hand. "Trust me, Jessie. Let's just enjoy our lunch and see what happens. I promise you, you won't get into any kind of trouble." Donovan let go of her hand and leaned back.

She looked into his eyes and saw that she could get into a lot of trouble with him if she wasn't careful. She forced a smile and wondered if she should have stayed firm and said *no* to lunch.

"Now that we're alone, tell me about yourself."

"I don't know if there's much to tell."

He tilted his head to one side. "What do you like and dislike?"

"I like the snow; I love having coffee with my friends, which we do about twice a week if we can. I like playing volleyball and I love children."

"You're the only Amish person I know. I'm considering starting an Amish restaurant. I know there are plenty around these parts, but I figure there's always room for one more. I'll make it bigger and better than all the others."

Jessie raised her eyebrows and wondered if that was why he had asked her to lunch, to find out more about the Amish. If so, she'd be disappointed. "How far have you gotten with your plans?"

"It's all in my head so far, that's all. What I figure is I'll have one side as an Amish market where people can buy Amish products, such as relishes and hand-crafted foods. The other side will be a family-focused restaurant. I'll be open all day from seven in the morning, and every meal will be large. What do you think?"

She put a hand to her mouth to cover a giggle. She couldn't help laughing at the excitement on his face.

He smiled. "What's funny?"

"It's funny to see you so eager about your ideas."

"I'm a very passionate person." He stared into her eyes so intently she had to look away. "Anyway, what do you think of my idea?"

"Seems good. I didn't know you were so interested in the Amish."

"I wasn't until I met you, and then I got to thinking about the Amish style of food."

She wanted to ask him his belief in God, but how would she approach the subject? Could she ask him straight out? "You seem to like our food, but what do you think of the Amish lifestyle?"

Donovan scoffed. "Do you want the truth?" Jessie nodded.

"I think it's completely ridiculous. Why would people keep themselves away from others? The children don't have a decent level of education, and you women are nothing but unpaid housekeepers and child-bearers."

Jessie was shocked at his vicious response. "I didn't expect you'd think such things."

He leaned in toward her. "It's a plain fact."

"Why would you want to open an Amish market and restaurant if you despise us?"

He leaned back in his chair. "It's about dollars. If people want that kind of thing, then I'll be there to provide it. I told you I'm going places."

"I don't like what you just said."

"Jessie, it's nothing personal. I just thought you might like the experience of going to lunch with a normal man before you get married and have ten babies. You Amish don't believe in contraception, you could have twelve children and ruin your figure." His eyes traveled down her body.

She stood up. "I don't care to eat with you. Goodbye." She walked to the door. Donovan sprang to his feet and followed close on her heels.

"Wait, Jessie, I'm sorry. I didn't mean it like that."

She asked the waiter, "Could you please call me a taxi?"

"Yes, ma'am." The waiter picked up a nearby phone.

Donovan waved his hand in the waiter's face while he said to Jessie, "No. I'll drive you back."

She turned to face him. "Finish your meal, Donovan, and you can have mine as well. I'll send you the money."

Donovan plucked a one hundred dollar bill from a thick wad he pulled from his pocket and threw it into the waiter's hands. He placed his hand on Jessie's elbow and ushered her out of the restaurant. "I can't tell you how sorry I am. My big mouth always gets me into trouble. I'm sorry I was offensive. I'll drive you back."

Jessie had been taught to forgive, so she accepted his offer to take her back to work. On the drive back, Jessie knew it was not *Gott's* plan that Donovan would join the community. How could she have been so naïve?

"Do you forgive me?" Donovan asked.

"I forgave you when you first asked me. I'm just shocked you think so little of my community. There's a lot more to us than those things you mentioned, and everything you mentioned is a benefit not a disadvantage."

"My biggest concern is, how can it be good not to have a proper education?"

"There's no point me trying to explain our ways to you and I don't wish to get into a debate. Tell me one thing though?"

"What?"

"Do you believe in God?"

"I have above average intelligence and no thinking person can believe those fairy stories about God and Jesus and all those things. It's not plausible."

"Who do you think made us, made the stars, the sun, the moon and everything else?"

"I suppose there could be some higher power, but I'm not about to believe something that I've not seen or experienced myself." They arrived at the B&B and he parked the car in the usual place. "Only a fool believes something he can't see, taking it by faith alone. Someone could make up anything and tell you to believe it by faith."

Things were going from bad to worse. "Donovan, you think of me as a fool?"

"No, that's not what I meant. I meant…"

"Best you don't explain." Jessie got out of the car and looked up to see Elijah standing there next to his *onkel*. She gasped for air, as it caught in her throat. "Elijah, what are you doing here?"

"I told you, I was doing some work with my *onkel*."

Donovan got out of the car. "Ah, you're the people I called for a quote? You're early." Donovan shook hands with both men and turned to Jessie, who was still standing there dumbfounded. "I'll see you soon." As he walked away with the two men, Jessie heard him say, "I didn't expect you so soon; I was just having lunch with my girl."

Jessie took a deep breath to still a wave of nausea that washed over her. This was not good. How could she explain the situation to Elijah? She stood near the car and watched the three of them walk away. Elijah glanced over his shoulder at her and then turned away.

Chapter Twenty-Three

The rest of the afternoon, Jessie did not see Donovan or Elijah. She wanted to explain to Elijah that she was not Donovan's girl. What would he think of her now? She had agreed to see him more and then he heard Donovan calling her "his girl" shortly after.

She couldn't go to Olive's house and tell her what happened because Elijah would be there. She had only been waiting one minute when she saw her father's buggy at the end of the road heading toward her.

On the ride home, she was grateful her father never had much to say. It allowed her to be alone with her thoughts.

Blake sat with his new friend, Ian Hilty. Ian was in his early thirties and helped work the family dairy. It was hard and grueling work and sometimes the stench was overwhelming. If he could just get through this period of testing then he would have the life he dreamed of with Olive. The community was the perfect place in which to raise Leo away from the harsh realities of the world. There was no better woman for him than Olive and he was pleased she felt the same about him.

Once he'd taken the final instructions, he'd be baptized and then he'd be able to marry Olive. He'd make a proper life for them. He'd been keeping his eye open for a suitable house whenever he'd had spare time. Secretly, he'd put a down payment on one and he hoped Olive wouldn't be upset with him when she found out. It was a surprise that he'd show her after his status as an Amish man was official, and then he'd propose to her properly. He thought about that day every night as he was drifting off to sleep. When he woke each morning, instead of thinking of the work before him, he'd be pleased because his new life had already begun.

Olive was careful not to visit Blake too often and they still couldn't be truly alone. It was permissible for her to visit him at the Hiltys' so that's what she did, knowing it was before the afternoon milking. When she pulled up in the buggy, she looked over and saw him sitting with Ian. She waved at them both. By the time she'd walked over to them, Ian had politely made himself scarce.

"Sit down with me," Blake said.

She was relieved to see he was still there and hadn't changed his mind about the whole thing. That was her secret fear. She bunched her dress in her hands and sat down next to him on the top porch step. "How are you?"

"Brilliant."

"That's good. And how's Leo liking it here?"

"Loves it. This is the perfect life for a child. He gets to play with all the baby animals, dig in the dirt, make mud pies and he's even been helping Mrs. Hilty with the cooking. He wants to help with the cows, but he's a little young for that even though he doesn't see it that way."

Olive giggled as she imagined Leo doing each of those things.

"He loves it here."

"And you?"

"I'm going through the motions here. It's a means to an end. Having a dairy is not the life I'd choose." He leaned into her. "I don't know how anyone does it."

"*Dat* and my brothers do it. It's what they've always done. You do what you have to do, I guess."

Noticing it was strangely quiet, she looked around. "Where's Leo?"

"Betty's taken him into town."

She hoped Leo would behave and not go running off like he had for his grandmother. "Have you heard from your mother?"

"I saw her last week. She still hasn't recovered from my decision, but she's pleased you'll be in my life."

"I'm in your life now."

He chuckled. "I know, but I meant when we're married."

A tingle of delight rippled through Olive's body. He still intended to marry her and stay within the community. "When do you start the instructions, have you heard yct?"

"Next week."

"Oh, good."

"Shall we go for a walk?" He sprang to his feet. "Let's."

Together they headed past the barn and into the cow paddock. "We will not have cows," he stated flatly.

She laughed. "You never want to see one again when you go?"

"When I leave here, you're right, I'll be happy if I never see one again."

"Okay, I'll remember that. I'm off to visit Jessie when she finishes work today. Maybe I'll wait until after dinner. *Jah*, that's what I'll do."

"How is she?"

"Good. I think. I haven't seen her for a while. She's working hard at her new job."

They walked a little further through the grassy fields.

"*Denke* for waiting for me, Olive."

She smiled on hearing him speak a word of Pennsylvania Dutch. It was another thing he had to learn if he was to communicate and feel comfortable with those in the community. "Of course I would. It's unbelievable that you'd join us. This was the very last thing that I thought would happen. I mean, when I first met you—"

"I was a jerk. I know. A total jerk."

Olive laughed. "*Nee*, you weren't a total one." She held up her hand, and placed her thumb and forefinger an inch apart. "About this much of a one."

He chuckled. "I don't know what would've become of Leo and me if you hadn't come into our lives. This is the perfect life for us, and I'm focusing on what's important for this life and eternity."

"I'm happy to hear it. I was hoping it wouldn't be too hard after you were used to so many luxuries. You could have anything you wanted."

"What I want is things that money cannot buy. Being right with God doesn't hinge on finances. What use is money when it all boils down? We can't take it with us."

It filled Olive's heart with gladness to hear him speak those words.

When Jessie arrived home, she needed advice and went in search of her brother. He was a man; he would know how they think. He had crutches now and was no longer confined to his room. She looked downstairs, but he was nowhere to be seen.

"Can you help me with dinner, Jessie?"

"*Jah, Mamm*, I'll be there in a minute." She raced upstairs and stuck her head into her *bruder's* room and saw him resting. "There you are. I need to talk with you."

His jaw dropped. "Again?"

"Don't be like that, Mark, it's important. Can we talk after dinner? I've got to help *Mamm* now."

Begrudgingly, he slowly nodded. "Okay."

She knew he was less than enthusiastic, but she had no one else. Jessie hurried away to help with the dinner and when she got to the kitchen *Mamm* was peeling the vegetables.

Mamm looked up at her. "How was your day? You look a little worried."

"I just had an awful conversation with my boss's son about *Gott* and the community."

"Don't let things like that upset you. Not everyone will believe."

"I know, but it wasn't like that. He said awful things about our way of life."

"He's entitled to think what he wants, Jessie. It's best to pay people like him no mind. He's an *Englischer*."

She wanted to explain how horrible Donovan had been, but didn't want to repeat the awful things he'd said.

"That's why we remain separate from the people of the world," her *mudder* added.

Jessie nodded as she sat down to shell the peas from the mountain of peapods.

When dinner was over and the kitchen cleanup done, Jessie followed her brother back up to his bedroom so they could speak privately.

He lowered himself carefully onto his bed. "Okay, what is it you want to tell me or ask me?"

She sat on the other side of his bed and faced him. "I had the most horrid day. The boss's son, Donovan, tricked me into going to lunch with him and…"

He raised a sceptical eyebrow. "How could he do that?"

She lifted her hand to silence him. "Let me tell you everything first and then you can ask questions."

"Go ahead."

"So, he tricked me by saying he wanted my opinion about a competitor's restaurant. While we were at lunch, I found out he's unethical, and he said horrible things about the Amish people as a whole."

"He's entitled to believe as he wishes."

"*Jah*, that's what *Mamm* said, but he was insulting to me. Anyway, I said I wanted to leave and then he drove me back to work, and we didn't even have lunch." She drew a breath. "When I got out of the car, who do you think was standing there?"

"His wife?"

"*Nee*. He's not married." Jessie laughed as she leaned over and hit his arm. "*Nee*, it was Elijah."

Mark lifted an eyebrow. "What was he doing there?"

"He told me yesterday he was going to start doing construction work with his *onkel*. I didn't know he meant right away. He was standing there with his *onkel*. They'd come to give Donovan a quote on building something for his *mudder*."

"That's not good."

"It gets worse than that." Mark rolled his eyes.

Jessie continued, "When they walked away, I heard

Donovan say he was just back from taking his girl to lunch."

Mark looked away from her and scratched his head. "That's definitely not good."

"He could've meant that I was 'his girl' because I work for his *mudder*."

"*Nee*, men say things like that to show ownership of a girl. It was deliberate. He would've seen the interaction you and Elijah had, and he didn't like it. I'd say Donovan wants you for himself." One eyebrow rose, just slightly, as he asked, "Have you given him any encouragement?"

"Really, you think he likes me? But from what he said, he despises the Amish."

"Did you give him encouragement? Answer me."

She wasn't quite sure what he meant. *Was sitting with him at lunch encouragement? Was asking him questions?* "*Nee*, I don't think so."

"Thing is, if he said that within your hearing, what would he have said when you were further away?"

Jessie gasped. "You think he's said something else to Elijah about me?"

"It's possible." Mark scratched his chin. "What were you thinking, going to lunch with Donovan when it's Elijah you like?"

Jessie looked down. He'd come to the same conclusion she had. "It was stupid. I know that."

"Do you like Donovan?"

"I did like him, I thought I did, but not now. I think he's horrid. He is handsome and all that, but he doesn't seem a *gut* kind of person. He's a bad person."

"I don't believe there's such a thing as a bad person. He might have made bad choices."

"*Jah*, a lot of them I'd say, and he's willing to make a lot more just to make money. That's practically all he talks about."

"If you hadn't gone to have lunch with him you wouldn't know all this and you wouldn't be so upset. It seems you might like this man more than you admit."

"Even if I did, where would that leave me? It's clear he'll never join us like Blake has."

"Blake's not fully Amish yet."

"He will be, though, as soon as he can. It takes time and he can't get baptized until the bishop thinks he's stayed with the Hiltys for long enough. He's well on the way."

"I hope so, for Olive's sake." Mark lifted his leg a little and stretched it out. "It's getting itchy under the cast."

"That means it's getting better. Anyway, what advice can you give me?"

"Don't be worried and leave everything in *Gott's* hands."

Jessie huffed and rolled her eyes. "That's easy for you to say, but what if there's something *Gott* wants me to do? Maybe there's something I've gotta do."

"Then He'll make it clear to you. Don't worry so much. It'll all work out. Have faith."

Jessie licked her lips. "Do you want me to tell you all the horrid things Donovan said?"

Mark frowned. "*Nee*, I don't want to fill my mind with that kind of thing, and you should do your best to keep it out of your head. The Scripture says to keep your mind on all that is pure and good."

"Okay." She stood up and patted Mark on the shoulder. "Can I get you anything?"

"*Nee*, I'll have a rest here for a while. But a word of advice before you leave."

"*Jah?*"

"Think of others before yourself. Don't be so consumed with your own problems that you're not there for those who need you."

Jessie nodded. "Got it." Jessie left her *bruder* and went down to help *Mamm*. As soon as she walked into the kitchen, the back door opened. She turned to see Olive. "Olive, come in."

Jessie's *mudder* said, "Hello, Olive. You've just missed dinner, I'm sorry."

"It's okay, Mrs. Miller. I've eaten. I just wanted a quick word with Jessie."

Mrs. Miller smiled. "I'll put the kettle on so you can have a nice cup of tea with Jessie."

"*Denke*, Mrs. Miller."

Mrs. Miller gave the table a final wipe before she prepared the tea, and then she left the two girls alone.

"What happened today?" Olive whispered.

"Have you been speaking to Elijah?"

"*Jah*, he won't talk about you. I asked him how the buggy ride went, and he said the subject of you is closed. I know he went out to where you work. I heard *Onkel* Henry and Elijah talking about possibly getting a job there."

Jessie bit her lip. She was a closed subject to Elijah. She'd gone full circle; she had no prospects of a husband, then she thought she had two, and now she was back to none.

"Well?" Olive asked.

"I'll get you cookies, or would you prefer cake?" Jessie pushed her chair out to stand up.

"Neither. Talk to me, Jessie. What's going on?" Olive took hold of Jessie's hand and pulled her back down in the chair.

Jessie took a deep breath and told her about Donovan, the horrible things he'd said and then seeing Elijah when she got back to the B&B. "Worst of all, Donovan made it sound like we were boyfriend and girlfriend. He was so convincing. I nearly believed him myself." Jessie sighed and put her head in her hands. "I've made a mess of things."

"Don't worry. Blake seemed horrible at the start, and I found out he was only that way for a reason. He was struggling with things from his past," Olive said.

"So, you think that Donovan might not be a horrible man? Is that what you're saying?" Jessie raised her head.

Olive licked her lips. "It's always possible. I'd love you to be married to my *bruder* but if you like this other man better, it's best you don't encourage Elijah. He deserves someone who believes he's the best."

Jessie breathed out heavily. She liked them both, and if what Olive said was true Donovan might be acting horrible for a reason. There could be hope after all. Maybe he didn't believe all those horrible things he'd said about the community. "*Denke* for coming to see me. I've not wanted to speak to you about Donovan because I know you want me and Elijah to be together."

"I still do." Olive gave a little laugh.

Remembering her brother's words, she didn't want to be a selfish friend. "How are Blake and his little son, Leo?"

"They're fine; they like the community, which is *gut* for me." Olive giggled, and her face flushed a shade of deep pink.

"It's nice you both found each other, and his little boy will have a *mudder.*" Olive nodded.

"How did you change him?"

"I didn't do anything. Well, not that I know of. He said he believed in *Gott* a long time ago and he always had thoughts of how we all got here and why."

Jessie knew Donovan had thoughts just the opposite. Was there any hope that Donovan would suddenly change his mind and realize that *Gott* was not a fairy tale? Jessie could not tell Olive that she liked both men in different ways for different reasons. She wouldn't understand. "I'm going to have some cake. Do you want a piece?"

Olive nodded, and Jessie could tell by the look on her face she was upset. Jessie cut two slices of plain cake, popped them onto plates, took two forks and then sat down again.

Olive moved the teacup closer to herself. "What's Donovan like?"

"He's very hardworking and that's one of the things I like about him." Jessie left out the terrible things he'd said at lunchtime. "He's tall, handsome, and his hair is cut short. He's got the cutest smile." While Olive bit into the cake, Jessie thought about the two men and compared them to horses. Elijah would be a draft horse, whereas Donovan would be a sprightly Standardbred. "Elijah and Donovan are both handsome." *Possibly the draft horse would be the more dependable,* Jessie considered.

Olive sighed. "It is a risk, you know, liking a man who's not from the community."

"I know, Olive." Jessie topped up Olive's tea even though she had hardly drunk any.

"Think how easy it would be if you married Elijah. He's from the same community, he doesn't live far away, and we'd be *schweschders*-in-law, and everything would be perfect. You have the same beliefs, and there's nothing stopping the two of you having a *gut* life together."

"Hmm. Except he said the subject of me is closed, didn't he?"

Olive swiped her hand through the air. "Never mind about that; I'm sure he was just upset. He won't be that way forever. I could speak to him if you like."

"*Nee*, don't do that. I'll just leave things in *Gott's* hands and see what happens. Tell me more about what's happening with you."

"I can't help being fearful about Blake. I mean, the hardest work of all is on a dairy farm." She shook her head. "I don't know why the bishop put him with the Hiltys."

"Are you worried the hard work will turn him off and he won't stay?"

"I am. He's used to long hours and everything, but being on a dairy is so different from everything else he's done. I just saw him today and he seemed good, so I feel a little more relaxed."

Jessie was thankful for her brother's advice when she saw her friend had troubles of her own. "He knows it's not forever. And, once he's finished his time at the dairy farm, he'll be able to live anywhere he likes once he gets baptized."

"I know. I've got no reason to think the way I do. I'm just not used to things going right for me. Everything seems too good to be true starting from the time I met Sonia and Leo at the farmers market."

"Are you waiting for something to go wrong?"

"I think so and then I feel awful for letting my mind run to dark places. I would be devastated if Blake and Leo left my life forever. There'd be a black hole."

"Most of our worries are about things that never happen, so don't worry."

"Easier said than done."

Jessie stared at her friend wondering what to say to encourage her. "If you married an Amish man, he could leave the community at any time as well."

Olive giggled. "Is that supposed to make me feel better?"

"Well, you laughed." Together, they giggled.

"You are right. I'll do my best to leave my worries with *Gott* and not take them back again."

"*Jah*, we should all do that more often." She looked down at Olive's teacup. "Your tea's getting cold."

When Olive went home, Jessie walked upstairs to her bedroom. Tonight, she was wearier than she'd been in a long time. After she changed into her white cotton nightdress, she slipped between the cool cotton sheets. Her eyes closed, and she wondered whether *Gott* wanted her to do anything or whether she should leave things be. So tired of thinking was she that sleep came quickly.

Chapter Twenty-Four

The next morning at work, Jessie was surprised to see Linda. "How's your ankle? I didn't expect to see you for weeks."

She looked down at her feet and then looked back at Jessie. "Fine, I guess. What do you mean?"

"Donovan told me you twisted your ankle, and he said you were taking a few days off."

Linda put her head to one side. "Strange for him to say that. No, he told me I could have the day off and it would be our little secret. Well…secret from Mrs. Billings since she wouldn't be at work. Now, you have to keep the secret too."

Jessie nodded after she realized Donovan had gotten Linda out of the way so it would be easier to talk her into going to lunch with him. She hurried to the cleaning room behind Linda and when they got there they saw Elijah crouched over, measuring one of the carts. Jessie stood still and watched, searching for words and hoping he wasn't angry with her.

He stood up, and then saw her. "Jessie."

"What are you doing here, Elijah?"

"My *onkel's* been given the job we quoted on. We're building an annex room onto the house for the cleaning equipment."

Jessie had forgotten Linda was there until she suddenly spoke. "I'm Linda."

Elijah nodded politely. "Nice to meet you, Linda. I'm Elijah."

Linda's face beamed as she stared at Jessie as though waiting for her to say something. Feeling Linda's eyes fixed on her, Jessie stammered, "Um, I suppose while you're here you might help us up the stairs with the carts? That is, if you're finished with them."

"Sure."

After he helped them get the carts up the stairs, Elijah went back to the cleaning room.

"Who's he?" Linda whispered, as they pushed the carts up the hallway.

"A friend."

Linda scoffed. "Bit more than a friend I'd say, the way he looked at you. You could cut the tension with a knife. Something was happening between the two of you."

Jessie pushed out her bottom lip. "What do you mean?"

"Sparks were flying; even my heart was racing."

She shook her head. "You must have imagined it."

Linda laughed at Jessie's response and was still cackling when they parted to clean separate rooms.

Jessie was glad Elijah was speaking to her even though he seemed standoffish. Maybe he had to speak to her because Linda was there listening to every word. This was her chance to explain why she had been in Donovan's car and tell him she was not Donovan's girl.

Mrs. Billings still hadn't arrived, so would it do any

harm if she slipped away to speak to Elijah privately? Jessie seized the opportunity and hurried back to the cleaning room and stood at the doorway looking in at him.

"Forget something?" Elijah asked.

She walked toward him. "I just wanted to tell you that I wasn't on a date with Donovan yesterday. We just had lunch, and that was all. Well, we didn't even get to have lunch, but that's a long story. Anyway, I heard what he said to you about me being his girl. I'm not his girl; I just wanted you to know that."

Elijah casually put his hands on his hips. "I don't want to mislead you, Jessie. I asked you on a buggy ride because my *schweschder* kept pestering me to take notice of you. She has it in her head we'd be perfect for each other. It's clearly not so. Wouldn't you agree?" He lowered his head waiting for an answer and his eyes remained fixed on hers.

She knew how convincing and forceful Olive could be. If she was nagging her *bruder* just as much as she'd been nagging her, no wonder he eventually asked her on a buggy ride. He couldn't have been clearer letting her know he wasn't interested. "*Jah*, I agree. I know how Olive can be. I'd better get back to work."

"*Jah*, me too," Elijah said.

Jessie hurried back up the stairs feeling heartbroken. When she reached the room where she'd left her cart, she closed the door and the tears spilled down her cheeks. He'd never liked her at all. Olive had forced him to take notice of her. She pulled a tissue from the box in the bathroom, wiped her eyes and then blew her nose. Once she had splashed cold water on her face, she decided it must all be in *Gott's* plan just like her *bruder* had told her. Maybe Donovan would change and become the man for her after all.

Lunchtime came and went with no sign of Donovan. At three o'clock, Jessie looked out the window to see Elijah and his *onkel* leaving. She moved closer to the window so she could see them drive up the road. Just as they disappeared, she saw Donovan's car speeding toward the B&B.

When she looked harder, she saw he wasn't alone. There was a woman in the seat next to him. With her heart thumping, Jessie watched as Donovan got out of the car, and then hurried to open the passenger-side door. The woman stuck out a high-heel clad foot, placed it on the ground and the rest of her followed. She was tall and willowy with long raven-black hair. Her slender figure was shown off by a figure-hugging black dress. From Donovan's smile, Jessie knew he was infatuated with her. Side by side, the two of them walked into his restaurant.

With two more hours to go, Jessie made a concerted effort to put Donovan and Elijah out of her mind while she cleaned. That afternoon, they were working on the insides of the windows.

"There you are," a familiar voice sounded from behind her.

It was Donovan and he was smiling. "Hello." She climbed down from her stepladder and wasted no time telling him what bothered her. "Yesterday you told those men I was your girl."

"I want you to be, that's why." He folded his arms across his chest. "What do you think about that?"

Jessie giggled, and her heart beat so hard she could barely breathe. "I can't be with someone who doesn't believe in *Gott* and from what you said you have no intention of joining the community." She drew a quick breath. "You also think deceiving people is all right and I can't be with someone like that."

He smiled, walked forward and put his hands on her shoulders. "All those things I said at the restaurant about deceiving customers was a joke." Frowning, he continued, "That's my sense of humor. I didn't mean to upset you so much. I'm sorry."

"What about the things you said about God?"

"No, that wasn't a joke."

Jessie was disappointed. "Who was that girl in your car when you drove up?"

He dropped his hands from her shoulders. "I'm not a monk, Jessie. I have needs."

Jessie gasped, and her hands flew to her mouth.

"I can still see you and get my needs met elsewhere; there's nothing wrong with that."

"No, I will have nothing more to do with you. I'll quit my job if I have to. Leave me alone."

He stepped back and studied her. "No, you don't have to do that. Be reasonable, Jessie."

"I don't want to talk about your needs. Now, if you'll excuse me I have windows to clean." She turned away and took a step back to the window.

"Jessie, you might be the girl I marry—eventually. If you play your cards right."

"No." She took her rag out of the bucket and climbed back onto the stepladder and polished the glass. She did not know when he left the room, but when she turned around moments later, he was gone. He wasn't worth all the excuses she'd made for him.

Chapter Twenty-Five

After dinner that night, it hit Jessie again what a fool she'd been to think she could make a relationship work with an *Englischer*. She was also embarrassed Olive had forced Elijah to show interest in her.

Jessie's father decided it was time they had a *familye* Bible reading. Glad of the diversion, Jessie read quietly while she nestled into the cushion at the side of the couch. She drew comfort from *Gott's* word and knew she'd feel even better after a good night's sleep.

When the time came to go to bed, Jessie followed Mark as he hobbled up the stairs. "Your leg seems better."

"*Jah*, it's not giving me any pain and I can put a little weight on it."

"Be careful. You don't want to break it again."

When he got up to the top of the stairs, he whispered, "What's wrong with you? You hardly said a word all night."

"*Ach*, can you tell?"

He nodded. She walked into his room, flopped onto the end of his bed and he sat next to her. "Well, go on, little *schweschder*. You might as well tell me because when this leg gets better I'll be too busy to listen to all your problems."

Jessie shook her head and looked downward. "I don't know where to start."

He sighed. "Sounds like another long story."

She took a deep breath. Jessie reminded Mark about her going out to the restaurant for lunch, and bumping into Elijah at the B&B. Then she told him about Elijah being forced into showing her attention. She told him about Donovan and the girl with the long black hair. "Donovan said he has needs. Then he said he might marry me eventually. What do you think of it all?"

"I'm too polite to tell you what I think, but I know Donovan is not the man for you. Do you still have feelings for him?"

Jessie wriggled. "I know he's not for me, but I kind of still like him if I'm honest with you."

"That's only normal. We can't switch our feelings off quickly. What we *can* do is choose someone wisely." Mark put his hand softly on Jessie's shoulder. "It's not enough that someone makes your heart race if they're totally unsuitable. Don't even allow yourself to think about someone like that."

A tear trickled down Jessie's face. "That was how I felt with Elijah. My head and my heart were right for him, but my heart was too caught up with Donovan, but not my head. Does that even make sense?"

"*Jah*, it does. Everything will work out. Things are already heading in the right direction since you're ruling out the *Englischer*."

Jessie nodded. "*Jah*, that's right, but Elijah never really liked me. I liked him a while ago and he never did anything about it, so I put him out of my mind completely. Well, I guess I did, until Olive started pushing him onto me."

Mark leaned back into his pillows and put his legs up on the bed. "What would happen if Elijah came to the door right now and asked you on a buggy ride?"

Jessie smiled. "That would make me happy."

"There's your answer then."

"It's not up to me; I can't do anything about it now." Jessie pushed out her bottom lip.

"Leave everything up to *Gott*, but at least now, you know who you want."

"*Denke*, Mark; you're a *gut bruder*."

Mark laughed. "Get out of here. I'm tired. I've got a big day of doing nothing but sitting around tomorrow. I suppose *Mamm* will find me something to do again. She usually does."

"*Gut nacht*," Jessie said, as she walked away.

After she was in her bedroom, she lay on her bed and her thoughts turned to Donovan and how he had manipulated things so they could have lunch together. She shut her eyes tightly and pushed him out of her mind. Her *bruder* was right; she would trust in *Gott* to bring her a husband. "*Denke, Gott*," were the last words on her lips before she went to sleep.

When Jessie got to work the next day, Donovan was waiting for her just inside the front doors. She looked at him, but hurried past without saying a word. He took hold of her by the arm when she was halfway down the hallway and swung her to face him. "Ow. You're hurting me, Donovan."

"What do you want from me?" Lines formed on his forehead.

"Nothing, nothing at all. I just want to come here, do my job and go home. I want nothing from you." She stared at his fingers wrapped around her wrist and then he released her.

"I was truthful. A lot of men would've lied to you."

She lifted her chin slightly. "I wouldn't have had anything to do with them either."

"Are you saying you're not interested in me because I told you the truth? Should I have lied?"

"No. I mean yes. I mean, I'm not interested in you. Telling the truth or lies is your choice to make. I'm Amish and you're not and it simply wouldn't work."

He narrowed his eyes. "You could leave the Amish, though. Then we could be together properly."

"I would never do that. I couldn't." Jessie shook her head. "Well, that's that then, is it?"

Jessie nodded and hurried to the cleaning room thinking that she'd rather be anywhere than where she was right now. Her *vadder* said she didn't have to work so maybe she'd be better off if she quit the job. But then she'd be a burden on her *familye* once again, and she liked being able to pay her own way. It made her feel grown up and responsible.

At lunchtime, rather than risk Donovan sitting with her under the tree, she went into town with Linda.

"Not having lunch with Donovan today?" Linda gave her a sideways glance as she clutched the steering wheel.

"No, we never had lunch together. I sat under a tree and he joined me."

Linda chortled. "If that's what you wanna say, then

good on ya. I did warn ya about 'im. I've seen many girls swayed by his sweet talk."

"I'm not one of those girls."

"How about if we go to the bakery? I'm feeling like a pie," Linda said.

"The bakery sounds good." Anything sounded good to her as long as it was far away from work and Donovan.

As they sat eating pies and cream cakes, Jessie realized the more she talked to Linda, the more she liked her. Time flew too quickly and then they were on the drive back to work. "I can't remember the last time I ate so much." Jessie patted her tummy.

"I thought you Amish folk ate a lot."

"We have a lot of food at our weddings and I guess we have a good spread of food at all our events. I'm usually helping though so I don't get to eat much."

"We need energy this afternoon because we're spring cleaning the kitchen from top to bottom."

"Sounds good. I like to have something to keep busy."

Linda pulled into one of the staff parking spots and they hurried into the building.

That afternoon, Jessie put all her energy into cleaning. Every time thoughts of Donovan or Elijah popped into her mind, she scrubbed harder. Fortunately, it was easy to keep her mind focused on other things especially since Linda kept talking.

Not long after she got home, she heard hoofbeats and looked out the window to see Elijah. She nervously licked her lips; he had to be there to see her. She went outside to meet him. He got out of his buggy and met her halfway to the *haus*. "This is a surprise, to see you." Jessie straightened her apron.

"I've come to tell you I wasn't truthful with you."
Not him too. "In what way?"

"I told you that Olive prompted me to see more of
you. The truth is that, well, the way I remember it is,
I'm the one who asked Olive what you thought of me."

At that moment, movement from near Elijah's buggy
caught her eye. She looked to see Mark getting out of
the buggy. Jessie frowned as she looked back at Elijah.

"*Denke* for driving me home," Mark said, as he made
his way past both of them. "Hello, *schweschder*," he
called over his shoulder as he hobbled on his crutches
up the porch steps.

Jessie was too shocked to speak. Had her *bruder*
divulged all her personal thoughts and feelings to Elijah? Is that why Elijah was now telling her the truth
and being so open? "My *bruder* has been speaking to
you about me?"

"Your name might've come up in conversation." His
lips turned upward at the corners. "Did I ever tell you
your eyes are a most lively shade of green?"

"*Nee*, you've never mentioned my eyes." Jessie's
heart pitter-pattered like it never had before.

Their moment was ruined when Jessie's mother
called out, "You'll stay for dinner won't you, Elijah?"

Jessie closed her eyes with embarrassment. Her
whole family was conspiring against her.

"*Jah denke*, Mrs. Miller, I will." He looked down at
Jessie, and said softly, "As long as that's all right with
you, Jessie?"

She wanted to know exactly what her *bruder* had told
him. She wanted to ask why he'd said he wasn't interested in her, but all that could wait. Looking into his

eyes, she silently thanked *Gott* for bringing him back to her. "It's more than all right with me."

They smiled at each other and walked into the *haus* side by side.

All Jessie remembered of dinner was eating shepherd's pie and hoping for a chance to be alone with Elijah afterward. After dinner, it was Jessie's father who suggested Jessie and Elijah have hot tea on the porch. From that, it was clear everyone knew why Elijah was there.

"*Denke*, Mr. Miller, I think we'd like that," Elijah responded to Jessie's father's suggestion while grinning at Jessie.

Jessie nodded as she rose from the table. Then she looked at her mother who would have to clean up by herself. As though *Mamm* knew what was on her mind, she gave a nod as if to say, "go ahead."

With cups of hot tea in hand, both Elijah and Jessie stepped onto the porch and sat down. Jessie found it hard to stop smiling and her cheeks ached. With no table separating them, they both placed their tea at their feet.

Elijah breathed out heavily. "It's another *wunderbaar* summer's night." Looking up at the stars, she was just about to agree when Elijah said, "Jessie, I acted like a fool when I saw you with Donovan Billings. I was mad with jealousy to see you in his car. I was even worse after the things he said."

"I understand."

"I need to ask you why you were in his car."

Jessie swallowed hard. Could she tell him that she had once liked both of them? Would he leave her if she told him the truth? "Elijah, you were not the only one who was a fool." She picked up her tea from the porch floor and looked straight ahead. "He kept asking me on a date, and I kept saying no, and then he asked about the lunch, which he insisted wasn't a date. I was silly enough to go with him after he assured me it wasn't a date, but still, I know now I shouldn't have gone." She sipped her tea, then turned and placed the cup on the table next to her, on the side away from Elijah. She turned back to face him. "I don't like him in that way. I liked him once, or I thought I did, but not anymore."

Elijah smiled and placed his hand on top of hers. "We all make mistakes. I made one two years ago when I chickened out."

"With me?" Jessie remembered the fun times they'd had at the volleyball nights and their long talks. She could never figure why he hadn't taken things further.

He took hold of her hand. "I terrified myself with visions of you saying 'no' to me. Then fear caused me to distance myself."

"Why is now different?"

He leaned into her and Jessie could smell his warm male scent, woodsy with a hint of sandalwood. "I'm taking a risk. My *schweschder* did have something to do with it. She gave me the push I needed. Mind you, she didn't know how I felt about you, I'm sure."

Jessie's body tingled when she looked down at their clasped hands.

"I love you, Jessie Miller."

Jessie looked deeply into his eyes. *He said love, not like.* She could feel the sincerity of his words and blinked back the tears that threatened to escape her eyes. "You do?"

He nodded, put his arm around her and squeezed her

shoulders. A loud throat-clearing from Jessie's father inside the house caused Elijah to pull his arm back.

Jessie giggled and hoped her father could not hear or see what was happening on the porch.

Elijah smiled and leaned close once more. "Will you be my girl, Jessie?"

Jessie sniffed quietly as a tear escaped and rolled down her cheek. "*Jah, jah,* of course I will." She looked at him and captured every detail, so she could remember the moment forever. The cool fresh air caressing her skin, the way she felt inside and how good it was to have a man like Elijah interested in her.

He smiled and leaned into her once more and gave her a quick, cheeky kiss on her forehead.

"Can I ask you something, Elijah?"

"*Jah,* anything."

"What did Mark say to you today?"

Elijah chuckled. "Let's just say some things are better left a mystery."

Jessie pushed her bottom lip out. "Aw, come on tell me."

He leaned into her again, and whispered in her ear, "He said I'd be a fool to let you slip away, and he wasn't telling me anything I didn't know already."

His warm breath in her ear caused her to giggle. She was pleased she had an interfering *bruder* and Elijah had an interfering *schweschder*, and she couldn't wait to tell Olive. Even though Elijah hadn't asked her to marry him yet, in her heart, she knew that would follow. Olive would marry Blake and she would marry Elijah. This was the happiest day of her life. Elijah put his arm around her shoulders once more and pulled her in close to him causing her to feel warm and safe. "I don't want you to work at that place again. I want to keep you far away from… *Englischers*."

"Oh." Jessie was delighted. It would be awkward facing Donovan again.

"Is that okay?"

"*Jah*, I'm happy with that. I'll give my notice."

"*Denke*. I'll help you find work somewhere else if you'd like."

"Okay, but I might want to take a break and help *Mamm* around the *haus* before I start looking for another job."

As Jessie rested her head on his shoulder, her mind drifted to Olive suggesting their small group of friends find jobs as maids and nannies. If they hadn't agreed, Olive would never have met Blake. And Jessie knew she had been meant to meet Donovan Billings because now she appreciated Elijah Hesh all the more. Now, she'd never take him for granted or wonder if there was anyone out there better suited.

Again, they heard Jessie's father clear his throat causing Elijah to edge away from her. Elijah and Jessie looked at each other and laughed.

It was becoming a habit that each of the five friends shared their good news at the coffee shop and Jessie sat at their usual table, early for the first time in, well, forever. She was the first of the girlfriends to arrive. Of course, Olive, being Elijah's sister already knew what she was going to announce, but the others had no idea.

One by one the girls arrived and when they all had their food and drinks in front of them, each shared her news, the good and the bad.

"And how's your job, Claire? You were worried about it last time," Jessie asked her.

Claire shrugged her shoulders. "I'm still there. Things are fine until the daughter-in-law visits. Nothing much has changed. The old couple and their son love me."

Lucy turned to Olive, "And what about you and Blake?"

"We're doing fine. I don't see him as much as I like, but he's doing well. Leo just loves the farm. It's better than being in front of a TV most of the time like he was with his grandmother." Olive then stared at Jessie giving her a nod, telling her it was time to talk.

"I have some news. Elijah and I are officially a couple."

All three of the other girls were in shock, much like when Olive had shared her news about Blake joining the community with his young son.

"Olive's Elijah?" Lucy asked.

"*Jah*. Elijah Hesh."

"You'll be Olive's *schweschder*-in-law," Amy squealed. Jessie nodded. "Maybe. I think so, in time."

"*Jah*, she will," Olive said.

Lucy looked at Olive and then Jessie. "We're all so pleased for you, Jessie. I don't know why we didn't think of Elijah when we were moaning about the lack of men around."

"I think it was because he's Olive's *bruder*. We just didn't think of him," Claire said. "Now that you two have men, it's our turn, isn't it, girls?"

"That's right," Amy said. "You two finding men gives us hope."

"It's something I want more than anything." Claire,

ever the romantic, clasped her hands to her heart, looked up at the ceiling and sighed loudly, causing all the girls to laugh.

"If it's happened for us two, it will for all of us. I just know it," Jessie said, and all the girls agreed.

* * * * *

Thank you for reading His Amish Nanny.
The next book in the Amish Maids Trilogy is Book 2: The Amish Maid's Sweetheart

SPECIAL EXCERPT FROM

Love Inspired®

Christmastime brings a single mom and her baby back home, but reconnecting with her high school sweetheart, now a wounded veteran, puts her darkest secret at risk.

Read on for a sneak preview of
The Secret Christmas Child *by Lee Tobin McClain, the first book in her new Rescue Haven miniseries.*

He reached out a hand, meaning to shake hers, but she grasped his and held it. Looked into his eyes. "Reese, I'm sorry about what happened before."

He narrowed his eyes and frowned at her. "You mean…after I went into the service?"

She nodded and swallowed hard. "Something happened, and I couldn't…I couldn't keep the promise I made."

That something being another guy, Izzy's father. He drew in a breath. Was he going to hold on to his grudge, or his hurt feelings, about what had happened?

Looking into her eyes, he breathed out the last of his anger. Like Corbin had said, everyone was a sinner. "It's understood."

"Thank you," she said simply. She held his gaze for another moment and then looked down and away.

She was still holding on to his hand, and slowly, he twisted and opened his hand until their palms were flat together. Pressed between them as close as he'd like to be pressed to Gabby.

The only light in the room came from the kitchen and

the dying fire. Outside the windows, snow had started to fall, blanketing the little house in solitude.

This night with her family had been one of the best he'd had in a long time. Made him realize how much he missed having a family.

Gabby's hand against his felt small and delicate, but he knew better. He slipped his own hand to the side and captured hers, tracing his thumb along the calluses.

He heard her breath hitch and looked quickly at her face. Her eyes were wide, her lips parted and moist.

Without looking away, acting on impulse, he slowly lifted her hand to his lips and kissed each fingertip.

Her breath hitched and came faster, and his sense of himself as a man, a man who could have an effect on a woman, swelled, almost making him giddy.

This was Gabby, and the truth burst inside him: he'd never gotten over her, never stopped wishing they could be together, that they could make that family they'd dreamed of as kids. That was why he'd gotten so angry when she'd strayed: because the dream she'd shattered had been so big, so bright and shining.

In the back of his mind, a voice of caution scolded and warned. She'd gone out with his cousin. She'd had a child with another man. What had been so major in his emotional life hadn't been so big in hers.

He shouldn't trust her. And he definitely shouldn't kiss her.

But when had he ever done what he should?

Don't miss
The Secret Christmas Child *by Lee Tobin McClain,*
available December 2019 wherever
Love Inspired® *books and ebooks are sold.*

www.LoveInspired.com

LIEXP1019

Looking for inspiration in tales
of hope, faith and heartfelt romance?

Check out **Love Inspired**® and
Love Inspired® **Suspense** books!

New books available every month!

SPECIAL EXCERPT FROM

Love Inspired®

*Carolyn Wiebe will do anything to protect her late
sister's children from their abusive father—even give
up her Amish roots and pretend to be Mennonite.
But when she starts falling for Amish bachelor
Michael Miller, can they conquer their pasts—and her
secrets—by Christmas to build a forever family?*

Read on for a sneak preview of
An Amish Christmas Promise *by Jo Ann Brown,
available December 2019 from Love Inspired!*

"Are the *kinder* okay?"

"Yes, they'll be fine." Uncomfortable with his small intrusion into her family, she said, "Kevin had a bad dream and woke us up."

"Because of the rain?"

She wanted to say that was silly but, glad she could be honest with Michael, she said, "It's possible."

"Rebuilding a structure is easy. Rebuilding one's sense of security isn't."

"That sounds like the voice of experience."

"My parents died when I was young, and both my twin brother and I had to learn not to expect something horrible was going to happen without warning."

"I'm sorry. I should have asked more about you and the other volunteers. I've been wrapped up in my own tragedy."

"At times like this, nobody expects you to be thinking of anything but getting a roof over your *kinder*'s heads."

He didn't reach out to touch her, but she was aware of every inch of him so close to her. His quiet strength had awed her from the beginning. As she'd come to know him better, his fundamental decency had impressed her more. He was a man she believed she could trust.

She shoved that thought aside. Trusting any man would be the worst thing she could do after seeing what Mamm had endured during her marriage and then struggling to help her sister escape her abusive husband.

"I'm glad you understand why I must focus on rebuilding a life for the children." The simple statement left no room for misinterpretation. "The flood will always be a part of us, but I want to help them learn how to live with their memories."

"I can't imagine what it was like."

"I can't forget what it was like."

Normally she would have been bothered by someone having sympathy for her, but if pitying her kept Michael from looking at her with his brown puppy-dog eyes that urged her to trust him, she'd accept it. She couldn't trust any man, because she wouldn't let the children spend their lives witnessing what she had.

Don't miss
An Amish Christmas Promise *by Jo Ann Brown,*
available December 2019 wherever
Love Inspired® books and ebooks are sold.

LoveInspired.com

Love Inspired®

Discover wholesome and uplifting stories of faith, forgiveness and hope.

Join our social communities to connect with other readers who share your love!

Sign up for the Love Inspired newsletter at **LoveInspired.com** to be the first to find out about upcoming titles, special promotions and exclusive content.

CONNECT WITH US AT:

Facebook.com/groups/HarlequinConnection

 Facebook.com/LoveInspiredBooks

 Twitter.com/LoveInspiredBks

LISOCIAL2019

WE HOPE YOU ENJOYED THIS BOOK!

Love Inspired® SUSPENSE

Uncover the truth in these thrilling stories of faith in the face of crime from Love Inspired Suspense. Discover six new books available every month, wherever books are sold!

LoveInspired.com

Love Harlequin romance?

DISCOVER.

Be the first to find out about promotions, news and exclusive content!

Facebook.com/HarlequinBooks

Twitter.com/HarlequinBooks

Instagram.com/HarlequinBooks

Pinterest.com/HarlequinBooks

ReaderService.com

EXPLORE.

Sign up for the Harlequin e-newsletter and download a free book from any series at **TryHarlequin.com.**

CONNECT.

Join our Harlequin community to share your thoughts and connect with other romance readers!
Facebook.com/groups/HarlequinConnection

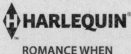

HARLEQUIN®

**ROMANCE WHEN
YOU NEED IT**

HSOCIAL2018